Don't Forget TO Write

LAURA DITIERI

Little Warrior Press

Don't Forget to Write
© 2025 Laura DiTieri

ISBNs
Paperback: 979-8-9999910-0-3
Hardcover: 979-8-9999910-1-0
Ebook and audiobook editions available.

Published by Little Warrior Press

Cover design by BE Designs
Interior design by Little Warrior Press
Edited by Julie Mianecki

Printed in the United States of America

First Edition, 2025

For my boys, who keep my heart full and my hands busy.

For my parents, who've carried me both literally and figuratively, with their love and unwavering support.

And always, my Matthew: you are my sunrise.

And most of all, you, dear reader (most people skip the dedication, so consider this my plot twist just for you).

Thank you—and happy reading.

"Hope" is the thing with feathers -
That perches in the soul -
And sings the tune without the words -
And never stops - at all -
- Emily Dickinson

Chapter 1

"Life is either a daring adventure or nothing at all." — Helen Keller

It's too hot, and this wool does nothing except make matters worse. Still, I need to look presentable. *Professional.*

Apparently, I decided wool on an August day was the way to do that. *Good thinking, Trudy.*

I smooth down the itchy fabric of my pencil skirt just to give my hands something to do. The matching blue blazer is tight and stiff in all the wrong places. *Ugh.* It's so hot—how is everyone else not melting? I try not to grimace and do my best not to fan myself like an old woman in church.

There are four other women here, all perfectly polished, their backs ramrod straight like they might snap in half. I have the sudden urge to sneak behind them and drop ice cubes down their blouses—just to watch the rigidity break. The image of them flapping and flailing like dancing chickens is almost too much. I bite the inside of my cheek to keep from laughing and have to clear my throat to smother the sound.

No wonder I want to be a teacher so badly—I'm nothing but a child myself.

I glance around the main office and my eyes land on a sign above the door:

Be Kind. Be Neat. Be On Time.

I can practically hear my father's accented voice reading it aloud, and the thought makes me smile.

"Miss Kirchberger? The principal will see you now."

I snap out of my little daydream and spring to my feet, heart doing cartwheels beneath my blazer.

"Thank you," I say, trying to sound demure, though the secretary barely looks up from her typewriter. She's typing away, fingers moving like lightning across the keys. The clacking is louder than it has any right to be—although I'm pretty sure my heartbeat is louder, which is saying something.

I step into the principal's office and take it in quickly. A massive wooden desk commands the center of the room, papers scattered across the surface, held down by several paperweights.

The cool relief of a metal fan hits me from the corner of the room and I briefly relish the feeling. Now I understand the need for all those paperweights—just as I hear the flutter of pages trying to make a desperate escape from their prisons. A black rotary phone sits on the side of the desk, its coiled cord dangling and dancing like it might leap off at any moment. Beside it, a giant coffee mug teeters dangerously close to the edge, making my eyebrows lift before I can stop them. Two large beige file cabinets flank his office chair, and above one of them, a dusty intercom speaker hums quietly, looking like it's ready to squawk out the latest cafeteria update at any second.

My eyes catch on a comically large framed sign that reads *Order is the foundation of success*, and I want to laugh at the irony. Just above it hangs a crisp photo of President Kennedy, and next to it, a fading photo of Ulysses S Grant.

So different from my last interview—with Sister Mary Immaculate (not her real name; Sister Eileen, I think— Sister Mary Immaculate is just what I call her in my head, thanks to her spotless desk and air of judgment). That one was at St. Agnes Elementary, which is still the front-runner in my book. It's smart to keep interviewing though. Keep getting my name out there. Keep showing up.

Back in the present, I hand the principal my résumé without comment, and slyly slide the coffee mug back from the brink. No need to let it ruin my carefully curated nightmare of an outfit.

I sit across from him, crossing my ankles and folding my hands neatly in my lap, ready for whatever questions he fires my way. He glances over my résumé briefly then adds it to one of the growing piles on his desk. His brown hair is tousled—evidence of how often he must run his hands through it—and there's a shadow of stubble along his jaw. My guess? He forgot to shave this morning.

"So, Miss Kirchberger, is it? Why do you want to teach?"

"Well, I love children and take the responsibility of shaping minds very seriously. I have a nephew and three nieces and watching them learn and grow has been such a joy in my life."

"You married?"

"No sir, not yet."

A nod. He liked that answer I suppose.

"Do you plan on having children?"

"I would love to. I love children, but as I said, I'm not married."

He furrows his brow, a flicker of distaste crossing his face, but he moves on quickly.

"Can you help with things like lunch duty, or extracurricular activities?"

"Oh yes, of course! I wear many hats," I gesture to the small one on my head and offer a laugh. "Always happy to lend a helping hand."

The questions continue until, at last, he stands to usher me out. I rise too. Before I leave, I look him in the eye.

"Thank you for your time. I would truly love the opportunity to work here. I'm smart, competent, and have a strong work ethic. I'm nurturing, but I can maintain discipline. I really hope you'll consider me."

His eyebrows lift slightly, as if surprised by the assertiveness. He gives a gruff nod and motions me toward the door.

I breathe a sigh of relief as I'm walking home. The air is thick with humidity and that unmistakable summer smell—the one that feels full of promise and like anything is possible. I cling to that feeling. Maybe I was too bold, but closed mouths are never fed. I know my father would prefer I be more reserved. I can't help myself sometimes, my mouth just has a mind of its own, and runs like a dog off its leash. I know that can get me into trouble sometimes, but it's the sixties for heaven's sake!

When I walk up to our Brooklyn brownstone and step through the door, the scent of apple strudel greets me, followed by the faint, familiar sound of humming from the kitchen. My mother does *so* love to bake, and I think— today especially—she's trying to put some good luck into the air, letting it mingle with the sweetness that's pouring from the oven. It's sugared, though not cloying, and I already feel the anxiety of the day falling off me like peeling off a jacket.

"Ma, I'm home!" I shout into the house, kicking off my kitten heels.

"My Trud-a-la! How did it go?" My mother's voice is so warm and full of love, lightly tinged with a German accent, and it eases a bit of my nerves from the outburst at the interview. I see the hope in her eyes.

"This *could* be the one. I have a good feeling, one of these will stick." I walk into the sunny yellow kitchen, head straight for the freezer, crack an ice cube from the tray, and pop it into my mouth. It's cold, clean, and exactly what I needed. I close my eyes and delight in its refreshing chill.

"What did you think of the school?"

"Very collegiate," I try to say, the ice now wedged against the side of my cheek. My mother rolls her eyes and turns back to her baking.

"Can you run to the deli and get some more cinnamon for me? I just ran out, and I'd like to make another batch for Mike, Annette and the kids."

I sigh. I *wanted* to take some time to cool off and overanalyze my interviews, but the mention of my brother, sister-in-law, nieces and nephew have me heading out, the screen door snapping shut behind me. The late-summer air presses close, thick enough to drink, laced with the scent of street pretzels and car exhaust. By the time I push open the deli door, the cool air hits like the Arctic against my skin—though it's probably only a few degrees cooler than outside. The store is small, its narrow aisles crowded with cans and boxes, the air steeped in the scent of coffee grounds and fresh bread.

I'm reaching for a tin of cinnamon when my hand brushes someone else's.

"Oh—sorry."

"No, please," he replies, voice smooth, amused. "You saw it first. Besides, how could I take cinnamon from a lady in what I assume is a cinnamon emergency?"

I laugh—too loud for the tight space.

"Is it that obvious?"

"Just a lucky guess," he says. "Or maybe I've seen that look before—determined, flushed, a little frantic. My mother wore it every time she baked for my father's business partners."

He's in his late twenties, maybe early thirties. Clean-cut, in shirtsleeves with cufflinks that somehow feel charming rather than showy. There's a calmness about him—a banker's confidence, maybe.

I can't help but take him in: he's tall, handsome, and unmistakably put-together. His white shirt is crisp and almost too bright. Blond hair neatly combed, brown eyes warm, with a few freckles dusting the bridge of his nose— just enough to hint at a boyishness he hasn't quite outgrown.

There's something about the way he stands—shoulders square, shoes polished—that makes it clear he's just come from work. And that he belongs to a world where things are orderly, dependable, and always just so.

He picks up the tin and holds it out.

"Here—take this one. On me."

"Oh no, really, you don't have to—"

"You'd be doing me a favor. Gives me an excuse to strike up a conversation."

I feel the blush creeping in and glance down. When I look back up through my lashes, he's still watching me. Our eyes meet and hold. The air shifts—thicker now, charged. He's handsome, yes, but it's the focus that gets me. Like I'm the only person in the room.

I clear my throat, a clumsy attempt to cut through the tension. "Well… thanks for the cinnamon. I should get this back before the emergency moves up to catastrophic levels."

"Of course."

"Thank you again."

"I'm Henry, by the way."

"Well—thank you, Henry."

"I hope to see you again. Maybe you'll tell me how this all panned out."

"Maybe I will," I say, holding up the cinnamon. "Duty calls."

Our eyes lock again, longer this time. Longer than necessary. And then I break it, stepping back into the sunlight, tin in hand and heart racing.

As I step outside, I blink against the light. The breeze hits my face and I realize how warm my cheeks are. I walk quickly, cinnamon tin gripped tight, though my mind lags behind—still caught in the quiet hum of the store, still feeling the weight of his gaze.

I round the corner and see my block come into view. The laundry lines ripple above, a group of kids chase a ball down the sidewalk, and Mrs. Lynette is sweeping her stoop like she's trying to scrub the whole street clean. It's all exactly as I left it—and somehow not.

Back inside, the scent of cinnamon and butter wraps around me like one of my mother's familiar songs.

"Did you get it?" my mother calls from the kitchen.

I hand her the red and white Frank's cinnamon tin and watch her measure it into the bowl like nothing's changed. Like I didn't just have the most cinematic five minutes of my life next to the canned peas and baking soda.

"Everything all right?" she asks without looking up.

"Yeah," I sigh, leaning against the doorway.

"Just... ran into someone."

"Oh?" Her tone perks up.

"Nothing," I add quickly, waving it off. "Just a guy being polite."

She hums in that knowing way mothers do and goes back to stirring.

I glance out the window. The sun is sinking lower, casting soft shadows over the sidewalk. Somewhere down the block, the deli bell rings.

And I wonder—just for a second—if he's still in there and maybe—for the first time—I feel excited about more than just the job.

Chapter 2

"Every new beginning comes from some other beginning's end."
—*Seneca*

Over the next few days, I keep finding excuses to walk past the deli.

Maybe I need milk. Maybe I just need air.

Really, I'm just hoping to see him again.

I know it's absurd—he doesn't live at the deli—still, the memory of that moment lingers, and I find myself hoping for more.

As it turns out, he had the same idea.

Because every day, there he is. Waiting outside.

Each day, we talk—just a little. And each time, I leave just as the tension starts to build. A pattern we both fall into, without ever discussing it.

Until about a week later, he finally breaks.

"So, my *cinnamon girl*," he says, grinning. "How about a real name?"

I smile, savoring the tease. "Oh, I *do* love a nickname. And who said I was yours anyway?"

He raises an eyebrow and smirks.

"Gertrude," I say, softening. "Trudy."

He repeats it once, mulling it over like a fine wine.

"Well, my cinnamon Trudy... how about we go out sometime? A drive-in, maybe? Or just coffee. I love our deli—it'll always be ours, of course—nonetheless, maybe we can branch out. See new places together." He gestures broadly around him.

I laugh, despite myself.

"I mean, I do love our place. It has everything you could ever really need."

"Hard to argue with the lady!" he calls into the street, loud enough to make two people turn.

I cover my face, laughing.

"Okay, okay," I say through my fingers. "Let me think about it."

He lets out an exaggerated sigh. "Well, I'll meet you at our place tomorrow."

I laugh again. "Is there anywhere better?"

"Don't think too long or too hard now, you'll give yourself a headache."

I flinch, just slightly, before reminding myself he's only teasing. "I'll be sure to carry aspirin at all times," I say, holding up my red leather coin purse to accentuate the point. "So don't you fret about how hard I think, Henry dear." I sing it sweet as sugar, wagging a finger for good measure.

He smiles good-naturedly. "Until tomorrow, then."

"Tomorrow," I echo, and start my walk home.

I've come to enjoy this routine and I'll be sad to see it end. I've enjoyed being the nameless cinnamon girl and the light banter we share on those hot August evenings. While going out on an actual date does have its appeal, I suppose, these fleeting moments of frivolity and lighthearted quips have been something I've begun to look forward to, and I'm not sure how I feel about it ending.

There's a kind of ache in knowing something good is slipping away, even if it's making room for something new.

Nostalgia rises in me like a tide crashing to shore, and looking around my room only deepens the melancholy. Boxes are scattered everywhere, filled with my belongings—little fragments of my life, carefully tucked away and neatly labeled. Each item has a place, and each place holds an item. If only life worked that way—organized, predictable, easy to understand.

In a strange way, it reminds me of my father. I see how much he likes things just so—neatly placed, in their proper spot. Organized. I'll miss them both when I move. We don't always see eye to eye on things and this is better in the long run but still... I know how much they both care. He would prefer I don't move out on my own, and my mind drifts back to when I told him I was moving away from our comfortable home in Brooklyn. I had been secretly looking for apartments in my spare time and finally locked one down that I loved. I was told it wouldn't be ready for a few months, but that worked out because I needed to tell my parents and get everything in order. Time feels like it has flown by since then, with the move-in date fast approaching. I remember it took me three different tries to muster up the courage, and broach the subject with my father. Thinking back on it now, the memory brings up a certain warmth.

"Dad, I've been thinking about it a long time. I found a place—not far, over in Queens. Just a small apartment, but it's mine. I'm going to move out." I say the last sentence with more intensity than I mean.

He pauses and frowns at me.

"Alone?"

"Yes."

"You think the world out there will be kind to you just because you're ready for it?" he asks, firmly.

"I know it won't be easy. I have to try though. I need to do this for myself. I'm a grown woman and I want to do things on my own. I *need* to." There is a pleading sound to my voice now; I just want him to understand. I have always had an itch for freedom and independence.

He looks out the window for a long time. I see his shoulders slump and he sighs.

"You have the key to the house. You understand? Always."

I smile warmly at him, the tension between us melting away like ice on a hot sidewalk.

"Du bringst Farbe in *mein leben, my Trudy.*"

He kisses my forehead and leaves the room without another word, the sound of the coins in his pocket the only sound.

Snapped back into the present, I sigh deeply and flop down onto my bed, exhaustion suddenly washing over me at the weight of the memory.

All this from being asked on a date? I think to myself. *Snap out of it, Trudy!* All of this is full of promise, of what tomorrow will bring. Maybe love, maybe I'll hear back from one of my interviews, and soon I'll be living in my *own apartment.* That's three good things to look forward to.

"Nothing but good times ahead," I tell myself out loud.

Until tomorrow, I echo again to myself, and drift off to sleep.

The next day I'm faced with a decision: do I take a visit to the deli and see Henry, or let the day pass and leave him hanging?

I spend the day lounging and catching up on *To Kill a Mockingbird,* but my mind keeps drifting away from the courtroom with Atticus and back to the deli.

I'm supposed to be immersed in justice and integrity, except all I can think about is Henry's grin and the way he says "our place."

I need to decide if I actually want to go on a date with him—or if I'd rather keep things just the way they are. Simple. Uncomplicated.

As I'm mulling over what to do, the phone rings abruptly bringing me into reality and out of the cycling of my mind. I run to answer it.

"Miss Kirchberger, it's St. Agnes Elementary School. We're very pleased to be able to offer you the position. You'll be placed in third grade and must report to the school on September second, right after Labor Day. We have several professional development days you are required to attend before the students arrive the following week. Do you have any questions?"

"No, thank you so much for this opportunity. I look forward to what the school year will bring!"

"We look forward to it, too. See you in September." *Click.*

I hang up, and feel a grin start to spread across my face. For a call that lasted all of two minutes, it just determined the trajectory of my life—for the foreseeable future, at least.

The job is mine. The apartment's almost ready. And Henry...

Well, he's still waiting.

I glance at the clock. It's not too late. If I leave now, I can still catch him at the deli.

I grab my bag, toss in my lipstick and a comb. Then, just for good measure, I add the aspirin with a smirk.

He's walking away by the time I'm walking up, so I add a little hop to my walk to catch up to him.

"Sorry, I didn't mean to leave you hanging," I say, slightly out of breath.

"I thought I scared you off yesterday," he says, almost sheepishly.

"No, I just got off the phone," I reply, brushing off his concern. "I was just offered a job teaching third grade." Pride threads through my words, making me stand a little taller.

"Wow." Genuine surprise seems to cross his face. "That's a very respectable job. You must be very smart. Those kids will be lucky to have you, until you're ready to settle down, of course." He smiles.

My mouth hangs open like a fish out of water.

"Oh good," I say, finding my voice, "I was worried I'd have to work forever. I'll go pick out my apron now. What color do you think matches my eyes best?" I joke, bat my lashes, and strike a pose reminiscent of Olive Oyl from *Popeye*.

He laughs, warm and full.

I feel my tension release. *He was just kidding Trudy, he's just teasing you.*

"Well, it seems a celebration is in order. How about we walk to the diner? Celebratory milkshakes—my treat."

"That sounds lovely," I say.

We step in sync into the thick summer evening air. The sun is just starting to dip, casting a golden glow over the street.

Henry walks a little closer than before, our arms almost brushing. I wonder if it's intentional, or just how wide the sidewalk is. He talks about his day—something about a new client, a possible merger—and I nod along, only half-listening, more focused on the sound of his voice than the content.

After a beat of quiet, he glances at me sideways.

"You know, I think it's admirable. The whole *teaching* thing."

He says it like a confession. A secret he doesn't want to admit.

"Not every woman's cut out for it. Patience, responsibility… You've clearly got both."

"Well," I say with a smile, "we'll see how patient I am once I've got thirty eight-year-olds staring at me. Now that I think about it, though, we've already seen how patient I am — I'm still here with you, aren't I?" I waggle my eyebrows and let out a small giggle.

He laughs. It's a nice sound.

We reach the diner. He holds the door open for me, and I catch the faintest look of something—approval, maybe? Admiration?

We slide into a booth, and as he hands me a menu, his fingers graze mine just a little too long to be purely accidental.

The menu's just a formality. In this kind of heat, milkshakes are the obvious choice—and the second he said it, I started to crave one.

"Chocolate or vanilla?" he asks.

"Strawberry," I say, folding my hands on the table. "I like to keep people guessing," I say with a wink.

He smirks like he wants to say something, but the waitress comes by, pad in hand. He orders for both of us—not in a controlling way, more like a movie scene he's imagined a dozen times. I let him. It's kind of nice, *just this once.*

When she walks away, he leans back and studies me for a second longer than I'm used to being studied, and it makes me shift uncomfortably in my seat.

"You know," he says, almost like he's thinking aloud and leaning back and folding his arms over his chest, "you've got a funny way of making someone feel like the punchline, or like an audience member of your life."

"I'll take that as a compliment." I say, although I hear my voice go up at the end like it's actually a question.

"Good. That's how I meant it."

There's a pause. Not an awkward one. Just the kind where maybe something could happen if someone dared to ask for it.

Instead, our milkshakes arrive. And we both smile like that's exactly what we were waiting for. The cool tang of the strawberry is divine, and I savor it for a moment.

We fall into our usual banter, and the evening carries a lightness that I've been craving.

We end up chatting for a few hours before I realize I need to head back. I'm moving in a few days and want to make sure everything is in order.

He walks me back to the deli, where we part ways with the promise that we should go out again. I think I'm actually looking forward to that.

It's the night before I'm moving into my apartment, and my mom wanted to have dinner together. We haven't done that in ages, and I thought it was a great idea.

She makes rouladen, one of my favorites, with a beet salad on the side. It tastes like comfort. Like childhood. Like days gone by.

I know it's our last real night here together, so I take a moment to really look at her, memorize her in this light, in this space. It's not forever, I know that. Yet these quiet nights, just the three of us, are drawing to a close.

I take in the soft gray creeping into her hair, the smile lines that have deepened over the years. Her kind blue eyes and round, familiar face. The apron tied around her waist, stained from an afternoon of cooking.

We're sitting in the bright yellow glow of the kitchen, laughing. It feels like joy. Like home. Like the part of me that will always be hers, no matter where I live.

I know Dad worked hard—she did too; I don't think she gives herself credit for everything she's done, I don't think anyone has if I'm being honest. She was here with me and Mike every day. She hugged us, sang our sorrows away, and protected me when Mike decided he wanted to be a little leaguer and practiced by throwing rocks wherever I happened to be. She made the house sing with joy and laughter. She was firm, but there was always kindness.

I'll miss the comfort of knowing she's here, making everything feel like home.

Dad starts in on one of his favorite stories from the bungalow, back when Mike and I were kids. It's in San Remo, over in Smithtown. They didn't want us spending our summers on tar beach. That's what we called the roof—hot, sticky, and smelling like asphalt—where families would lay out towels and pretend it was Jones Beach. So, they built a bungalow just a few houses from the water.

Dad saved for years to afford that small plot of land, and then he and his friends built the house with their own hands. I can't fathom how hard that must've been during the Depression, but somehow, he found a way. He always says he was one of the lucky ones—well, luck *and*, as he likes to remind me, "a strong work ethic, Trudy. Food doesn't pay for itself, you know, and nothing is guaranteed—not even a paycheck. So you have to work hard and prove that you deserve it." I internally roll my eyes at the lecture I've been fed a million times—still, he *did* hold a steady job at a grocery store when so many others were out of work.

I think that's what gave him the drive to start his vending machine business, and to build that bungalow.

It wasn't much, a small house with bunk beds, a narrow front porch where Mom and I would sit and talk about our day, a hand-pump for water that left my palms blistered, and an outhouse you had to walk to no matter the weather. The exposed wood inside was rustic and warm. The whole place was tucked beneath the trees, our own little private escape. It was just a short walk to the beach, so everything always smelled faintly of saltwater. Maybe it was the simplicity that made it feel so special. Either way, it created a little bit of magic, hidden behind the trees like a secret only we knew.

When I think about those summers, the memories sparkle. They're full of joy and laughter and sand in places no sand should ever be.

"*Ugh*, Mike was such a little devil," Mom laughs.

"You were my angel," she adds, winking at me.

I snort out a laugh, then Dad agrees all too quickly. "Yes, thank God for you. I swear he had horns and a tail! And you—well, you had the shiniest halo."

He launches into the story about the playhouse he built in the backyard. I *loved* that playhouse. Now the kids use it, and he gets the biggest smile watching them play, like the years folded in on themselves and gave him that joy all over again.

He's softer with them. I think that's a grandparent's job, though. With me, he still feels like he needs to protect, to guide, to worry. But with the grandkids—he gets to just be jolly and fun. No pressure, no expectations. Just joy. And he's so good at it.

I take the time to really look at him then too, like I'm trying to etch him into my mind. He's wearing that tweed flat cap he always favors, the one that somehow makes him look both distinguished and mischievous. His face is mapped with smile lines—deep grooves carved from years of laughter and letting the moment crease across his skin without shame. But there's a hardness too, just beneath the surface. The kind that forms from living through the Depression, from carrying too much too young, from shouldering the quiet weight of a family in a world that didn't always make it easy. I wonder what it must have been like—to leave everything behind and immigrate from Germany in hopes of a better life, only to be hit by the Great Depression and then, from afar, watch the place you once called home twist into something unrecognizable. To marry the love of your life on Ellis Island, dreaming of a bright future, and then work and struggle through years of hardship just to build the version of that dream you could manage to hold onto. All to fight the land of your birth— because it was the right thing to do, even if it meant turning against the home etched into your bones, poisoned to its roots by one man's madness.

I try to imagine sometimes what he saw, what he still carries, and how much he's tried to shield the rest of us from it. Maybe that's why he laughs so easily now. Maybe when you've seen real hardship, you learn to grab onto joy and frivolity wherever you can find it. Maybe that's how they both survived it all—by learning how to hold on tight to the good and let it ring out loud. I realize I've drifted off in thought and tune back in. Dad is chatting animatedly, halfway through a story about one of his vending machines. He had to refill two of them this week—one with candy, one with toys—and now he'll be heading down to Burch Street earlier than planned to replace a part in the candy machine.

I smile and listen.

Then I sigh, deep and content. I'm going to miss nights like these.

Chapter 3

"It takes courage to grow up and become who you really are." —
E.E. Cummings

It's finally time to move into my apartment—it's ready, and God knows, so am I.

I asked my brother to help me move, and he said he'd bring a few able-bodied men along. I could use all the help I can get. I'm frazzled—running up and down the stairs, hauling boxes, trying to figure out how everything's supposed to fit into this tiny space. Was it always this small? It felt bigger when it was empty.

I'm sweating more than I care to admit. I swear, this must be the hottest day of the year. As I'm in the middle of wiping sweat from my forehead, I hear the door open.

A tall, calm guy steps inside, with a dolly in one hand and a sandwich in the other.

He's so strikingly handsome, it's like he's sucked the air out of the room. Dark hair, just tousled enough to look effortless, and eyes a sharp, surprising blue.

I become acutely aware of the hair sticking to my neck, the sweat dripping down my back, and the unfortunate truth that I currently resemble a disheveled rag doll. The juxtaposition is almost comical—he's calm, collected, and impossibly good-looking.

I'm… well, let's just say a lady wouldn't dare say out loud exactly how she looks right now.

"You're not my brother," I say, eyeing him.

"Nope. Just the guy who owes a favor," he replies. I see a smile trying to sneak past his lips as he takes in my appearance.

Then—like it's nothing—he lifts the dresser I've been wrestling with for twenty minutes.

"You got a name, *guy who owes a favor?*"

"Frank. And now you owe me one, too." Then a full-blown smile escapes his lips. And it's the most beautiful thing I've ever seen.

"So, Frank," I say, arching an eyebrow at him, "are you in the habit of just waltzing into women's apartments?"

"I wouldn't say I waltzed." He pauses, considering, then nods at the dresser. "Well… maybe a foxtrot with that dresser over there. A very manly one, of course."

I don't want to laugh. I try not to. It escapes before I can stop it—a short burst of surprise that turns into a real, full laugh. "Very," I say between laughs.

Right then, the door swings open and Mike barrels in, looking like a cross between Johnny Cash and James

Dean—something I'm well aware is fully intentional, despite the "I don't see it" act he always puts on, but he always says it with a smile. He's been trying to slick his dark hair back like Cash for weeks, but the curl in it always wins out, leaving him looking more like Superman. I've been calling him James Cash lately. He doesn't find my refined sense of humor nearly as amusing as I do.

His brown eyes sweep the room, taking everything in with that piercing, overly serious expression that shows he's deep in thought. People who don't know him might assume he's intense—or slightly terrifying—really, he's the biggest softy you'll ever meet. My parents love to tell stories about how he used to torment me when we were kids, but I happen to think he got it all out of his system early. These days, he's more likely to show up with a toolbox, advice I may not always have asked for, and a threatening glare for anyone who looks at me wrong.

We squabble, of course—we're siblings—but if I ever needed someone in my corner, it was him. And here he is today, helping me move… and, let's be honest, probably inspecting the locks with an eagle eye and checking for structural weaknesses while pretending he's just "looking around."

Our mutual friend Petey is standing beside him, and I give him a wave and a friendly smile.

"Oh good, you're here already. Trudy this is Frank, Frank—my sister Trudy."

"We just met… seeing as he let himself into my apartment."

Mike shoves into his shoulder, "I feel like I shouldn't have to say, when you're helping, don't scare my sister. That feels like the opposite of helping."

"I wasn't scared," I say, lifting my chin. "I sort of deduced he was with you given the dolly in his hand. Unless he's a very helpful thief."

Mike shrugs. "I don't know all that much about him, if I'm being honest. He's Petey's friend. And Petey owes me and Frank owes Petey…. So here we are, but he's strong and if it means I have to lift fewer boxes, then I'm glad he's here."

"So you're saying he *could* be a thief? *And* that you're lazy. That's a lot to take in, Mike, and in such a short time!"

He grabs a balled-up newspaper from one of the boxes and throws it at me, but it drops unceremoniously to the floor right in front of him. We both laugh.

"Welcome to my place, Mike," I say grandly, spreading my arms wide.

He crosses the room in two big steps and pulls me into a huge hug.

"I'm so proud of you," he says softly, and I feel my throat tighten.

"Okay, okay—enough sentimentality!" I clap my hands. "To work, boys!" I laugh.

Frank laughs louder than the others and the sound is rich like honey. It wraps around me and I want to sink into the sound.

They scatter around the messy apartment as Mike starts snapping orders like he's running a moving crew. I head into the kitchen and rummage through one of the boxes until I find the lemonade mix, a pitcher, and a few glasses.

I make quick work of it—stirring, pouring, icing it down— then chug a glass myself before setting out the pitcher for the boys. If they're going to survive this heat, they'll need it. Thank God I had the sense to slide that ice tray into the freezer the minute I walked in.

I hear them putting together my bedroom set, and then footsteps come into the kitchen.

Frank.

"Here—you must be so hot." I hand him the lemonade, the sound of the ice clinking like music between us.

Our hands brush for a second. Nothing dramatic, just enough to make me notice how steady his seem to be. How easy he makes everything look.

But there's something else—something real. A flicker of electricity. I feel it shoot from where his fingers met mine, and I pull my hand back instinctively, surprised.

He doesn't say much, but he glances at me, and there's something there—like he's still cataloguing me, piece by piece.

"You okay?" he asks, with a soft chuckle.

"Yeah. Just… realizing I own more books than furniture." Shaking off the feeling. Obviously, the heat is getting to me.

He grins. "Could be worse. You could've made me carry a piano."

I laugh, loud and free. Already finding the conversation comfortable.

He lifts the glass, takes a sip, and says it with a casual kind of ease—like it isn't meant to knock the wind out of me:

"Plus, I kind of want to see all the books you're hiding in those boxes. Brains, boxes, and bravery. Dangerous combination. I bet you have men falling at your feet."

I blink at him. And then actually laugh—like a real one.

"Oh, sure. I have to beat them away with a stick," I say, rolling my eyes. "Must be all those cardboard boxes and sweat, completely irresistible."

I try to brush it off as a joke, but I feel the heat rising in my cheeks anyway. I know he's just being nice. Friendly. That's his whole thing—he's calm, he's *charming*, he helps people move dressers. Guys like that don't flirt with girls like me. Not seriously.

I look at him—and he looks right back. Our eyes lock, and for a second, everything else fades. Just us, suspended in this moment in time.

"FRANK! We need your help here!"

Mike's voice breaks through the moment like a snapped string. We both blink, like we've just woken up.

Frank sets the lemonade down, offers me a small, unreadable smile, and walks out to the other room.

I exhale—long and slow.

Okay. Definitely the heat. Or maybe I somehow managed to spike the lemonade.

After they all leave the space feels empty, but not in a lonely way. I look around slowly, letting it all sink in.

I step out onto the balcony and let the warmth of the sun settle on my skin. A wobbly little side table holds my glass of lemonade, condensation dripping down like it's melting into the metal, pooling under the glass. I pick up *To Kill a Mockingbird* and let myself sink into the chair, claiming a few quiet moments in my very own space. I look out over the balcony railing and take in my new view: rows of brick homes with laundry lines slung between them, like the whole block is airing its secrets. Late-summer roses pushing up in little gardens. Kids weaving on bikes so close they're bound to clip each other sooner or later. In the distance, the elevated 7 train rumbles by—a lullaby of the city, its silver cars flashing in the sun.

Across the rooftops, a faded billboard for Lucky Strike cigarettes looms above a corner pharmacy—some grinning man tipping his hat, a curl of smoke trailing from his lips like he knows something I don't. Below, a Coca-Cola sign glints in a diner window. A man on the corner hoses down the sidewalk in front of his deli, and somewhere nearby, a radio plays Sinatra, low and crackly.

It isn't glamorous. Nonetheless, it's brimming with life—and it's mine.

With Labor Day weekend coming up, I decide to take the week to adjust to my new place. It's small, yes—still I feel so much pride looking around my little place. I scrimped and saved and finally here I am. Starting my new job next week and on the precipice of so much promise. I've been putting everything away piece by piece, arranging and rearranging like it might help me settle my nerves along with the furniture.

The books go first, of course. I line them up on the shelf with quiet satisfaction—some standing straight, some stacked sideways—and then set up my desk beside them, where I'll do my lesson planning. It's a modest little corner, but it feels like the start of something real.

With everything in place, the apartment finally feels like it belongs to me—quiet, sunlit, and humming with possibility. I've had more time to think, to settle, to make little calls just because I can.

Henry and I have spoken a few times—light, casual calls full of banter and harmless teasing. It's nice. Easy.

Somewhere between organizing the silverware and folding dish towels, I start thinking about my sister-in-law Annette. I missed her after seeing Mike and want to catch her before summer's end. I call to ask how she'd feel about hauling the kids into the city for the day—maybe a trip to Coney Island.

She sounds excited by the idea. "That sounds like fun, I bet Michael Junior will spend the whole time trying to figure out how all the rides work." She laughs to herself, the kind of quiet, knowing laugh only a mother gives. "That boy... he's just so smart."

We chat for a while. She tells me how she's planning to make new outfits for the kids' first day of school and has already started gathering material to sew them. I can picture her pinning fabric to the dining room table, baby Denise sitting on her lap, Michael Jr. rattling off facts about sewing machines like an encyclopedia.

We make a plan. They'll come out on Sunday, and we'll all ride over together.

One last day of summer before the school year begins.

Coney Island is loud, sticky, and perfect.

It feels a little strange, seeing Mom and Dad now that I'm not living at home.

Strange isn't quite the word—the feeling is hard to put my finger on. It's a mix of sadness, and relief. There's a shift I can't name.

When they spotted me, they hugged me like I'd just come back from a decade overseas, not from a few boroughs over. I felt my throat tighten at the familiar weight of their arms around me. They smell like home and something familiar.

I miss them. I miss the quiet routine of being home—the comforting nothingness of it.

Dinner together, laughing over everything and nothing. Hearing about Dad's day at work or catching a whiff of whatever Mom was stirring on the stove.

Listening to Mom talk to Mike on the phone, then calling him myself and pretending I didn't already know what he was going to say.

There's a comfort in that rhythm—a sweetness to being known so deeply, so automatically.

And yet... there's a quiet ache, too. It's hard, being somewhere between child and adult in their eyes. Maybe I'll always live in that in-between. Then again, I suppose the backdrop of Coney Island and the cotton candy in my hand don't exactly scream "I'm a grown-up."

So maybe that part's not entirely their fault.

Theresa runs up to me then, snapping me out of my reverie by tugging at the hem of my skirt with one hand and pointing to the carousel with the other. Karen has both hands full of popcorn, offering zero explanation for the glittering streamers now tangled in her hair. Denise is perched on Annette's hip, drowsy and pink-cheeked, her blond curls damp from sweat and ocean breeze. And Michael Jr.—eight going on eighteen—is too cool for all of it. Which is why, of course, he's the first to sprint toward the Tilt-A-Whirl when Mike buys them all ride tickets.

"Slow down!" Annette calls, but she's laughing as she says it. "The ride will still be there whether you're running or walking."

"Speak for yourself," Mike mutters with a grin. "He's probably already calculated how many rotations it makes per minute. That boy's trying to beat gravity."

I lean into the moment, slipping off my sandals and feeling the sun-warmed boards of the boardwalk under my feet. The salt air tangles in my hair and mixes with the smell of popcorn, sunscreen, and hot dogs. I glance over at Mike and Annette and smile inwardly. The contrast between them is almost comical—he's loud, stocky, and takes up space like it's his job; she's small, soft-spoken, and has the posture of someone who's spent her whole life trying not to take up any. Don't let that fool you—when she believes in something, she digs in. Her frame is slight, her hair a pale blonde, eyes a bright blue—basically the opposite of Mike's darker features and deep brown eyes. And yet, somehow, it works. They balance each other. Always have. Like a marching band and a lullaby, but… married.

She catches me looking and makes her way over.

Annette shifts Denise to her other hip and sidles up beside me for a moment of calm in the swirl of popcorn, prizes, and chaos.

"She's out cold," she whispers, nodding to the baby's flushed cheeks.

I reach over and brush a damp curl off Denise's forehead. "She looks like a little angel."

Annette chuckles, tired and simultaneously content. "This was a great idea. I forget how fun it is when we're all together—and how much more fun it is when you're here."

I feign offense. "Forget how fun I am? And here I thought we were friends."

We both laugh—the kind of laughter that's earned through years of friendship, where you don't have to worry about how you look or how loud you sound. We sit in comfortable silence, just taking solace in each other's presence, watching the kids run around.

Then she turns and looks at me with quiet sincerity.

"I'm proud of you, you know. For doing this on your own. For moving out, starting fresh. I know it must be scary but, you have always just taken things head on. You've always had that spark."

"Well just call me a diamond," I joke.

She laughs again. "See? Sparkly," she says and waggles her fingers.

I laugh then look at her. "I don't see it as scary, to me it's a new adventure—and what's life without adventure? I've always wanted to live on my own and do things my way. No time like the present, right? Why do I need to wait for a man to marry me to live on my own? Why can't I just have my own space? Women are fully capable of having it all, if only we reach for it."

Annette smiles indulgently at me.

"Speaking of brave," I say tentatively, "have you gotten anywhere in the search for your natural mother?"

She exhales, long and deep. For a moment, she doesn't answer, just stares out, watching the kids play.

"No," she says at last, her voice low. "I haven't. I'll keep trying, I suppose. Little steps, wherever I can, you know? It's hard—knowing she's out there and I can't reach her. Maybe that's part of why I love having this family so much. Being a mother... it came easy to me. It always felt right. It made sense. And in some ways, it's made me miss her more. I can't help thinking—wouldn't she want to be part of this?"

She pauses, blinking up at the sun.

"I might stop looking for a bit, though. Just enjoy this stretch of life. I remember what it felt like, being young and feeling lonely. I don't want these kids to ever feel that."

"I'm sure she would," I say gently. "And it's okay to take a break. When you're ready to start again, I'll help however you need."

Except I'm not sure. I know this is a tender subject, and I'm not always sure how to be there for her—not in the way she might need. Maybe it's something I'll wait for her to bring up next time—when she's ready. I'll be here when she wants to talk—either way, I won't push.

And just like that, one of the kids shrieks with joy and the carousel bell rings, and the moment is swept away in a wave of motion. It snaps us both back into the present.

"This was a great idea," Mike says, walking over and looking at the kids. "I don't know who's having more fun." He tilts his head toward our parents.

I glance over. Sure enough, our father is standing by the edge of the boardwalk, holding a cherry Italian ice and grinning from ear to ear. He lifts his hat to reveal a tiny dancing flower perched underneath, sending Karen and Theresa into fits of giggles. With a small, proud flourish, he hands it to Theresa, then pulls another from his pocket and drops it into Karen's waiting hands. They squeal and clap, turning their new treasures over in delight.

I'd blame the silly toys on the Coney Island frenzy, but the truth is, he's always doing stuff like this. The kids can't help but flock to him. With his full laugh and the way he actually sees kids, rather than looking through them, it's no mystery why. You'd think he was made of candy, the way they stick to him.

Beside him, my mother fans herself, laughing indulgently as she accepts a pretzel from Michael Jr.

Karen runs over and shows me the new toy.

"Look!" she beams.

Annette grins at me.

"It's beautiful," I say, and hold it up like it's the most wonderful prize I've ever seen.

Suddenly, a blast of music signals the start of the next carousel ride, and the kids swarm toward it. Annette follows close behind, corralling them with ease, while Mike holds back with me.

He gives me a long look.

"How's the new apartment?" he asks.

I nod. "It's perfect, I've been liking having my own space. I've just been taking the time to get organized and really make it feel like my own."

"Do you feel safe there, on your own?"

"Mike! Not you too."

"What, you need to be prepared for anything," he says matter-of-factly.

I sigh. "Yes, I feel safe."

We stand there a moment, just the two of us, watching the blur of colors and shrieking joy as the carousel spins. Somewhere behind us, someone's shouting about fresh corn dogs and cold lemonade, but neither of us really registers it.

The sun starts to dip lower in the sky, casting a golden shimmer across the boardwalk. For a moment, everything feels suspended—the laughter, the breeze, even the ticking clock of summer—all pause while I take this second to inhale deeply, and I make a point to try to hold onto the feeling.

Then somewhere behind us, a familiar laugh carries on the wind. The sound is so familiar and warm and caresses my skin like a memory I didn't know I'd been holding onto.

I turn to the sound at the same time Mike registers a group of friends and waves largely at them. My eyes immediately find Frank in the group, only to find him already looking at me with a grin.

Mike waves a hand in front of my face, breaking our eye contact.

"Hellooo," he says in an exaggerated tone, grinning.

I blink, caught, and try to play it off.

He raises an eyebrow, then lets the moment pass with a smirk.

"Come on," he says, nudging me gently. "Let's go say hi."

We walk over to a large group—some familiar, some not. I spot Petey right away, and Mike claps his hand in greeting. He's standing beside Frank, who catches my eye as I wave.

"Thank you again for helping the other day," I say, aiming it at both of them, but feeling Frank's gaze linger.

To my surprise, Patty and Caroline are here too—two of my oldest friends. I haven't seen them in weeks, and it's like a little reunion in the middle of the boardwalk chaos.

We slip into easy chatter, catching up between bites of cotton candy and calls from the kids. I fill them in on the new job, tell them they're officially invited to my new place for coffee and gossip—"Bring folding chairs if you must." They hassle me that the boys have seen it first, and of course, Henry comes up.

"It's casual," I say quickly, but I can already see their expressions lighting up—like bloodhounds catching the scent of something juicy.

They ask what he looks like, what he does, if he drives a fancy car.

"I don't really know what he does," I admit, laughing. "Something about mergers. Sounds serious." I furrow my brow, throw on a mock-serious face. "Very important, I'm sure."

They burst out laughing and I find myself relaxing, slipping back into that familiar rhythm of teasing and girl talk.

The carousel bell rings again, and Theresa comes bounding over, tugging at my hand.

"Aunt Trudy, ride with me! Please?"

The others keep chatting, but out of the corner of my eye, I see Frank crouch down to her level.

"And what's your name?"

"Theresa," she says proudly, sticking out her chest. "I'm four years old." She flashes four fingers like a badge of honor.

"Whoa! You must be headed to work soon, huh?"

"No! I'm going on the carousel!"

"Well then," he says, eyes twinkling, "you must be very brave. That ride would make me dizzy."

"I'm *the bravest*. But you won't get dizzy. You can try it."

She tugs my hand again, and I let her pull me toward the painted horses. I choose a gold-and-cream mare, and she picks the one beside me.

To my surprise, some of the guys follow and climb onto the horses behind us.

The carousel lurches into motion, and the music swells around us—loud and sweet and strangely nostalgic.

The wind whips my hair, and I glance behind me. The guys are laughing at something, happy and carefree. Frank catches my eye and tips his hat.

A teasing smile playing on his lips—like he sees something I haven't figured out yet.

I look away, but I can't stop the grin tugging at the corner of my mouth. The horses go up and down. The lights blur.

And for a moment, everything—summer, new job, pressure, expectations—melts into the hum of music and a pair of quiet, curious eyes.

We walk back over to where Mike and Annette are standing, just as the first low boom of fireworks echoes in the distance.

"Let's do one last ride before they start," I say, glancing at the sky.

"How about the Ferris wheel?" Mike offers. "If they go off while we're up there, we won't miss a thing."

We all agree and head over as a group, weaving through the crowd toward the bright, creaking wheel.

Annette stays back with Denise on her hip, bouncing gently to keep her content. Michael Jr. says he wants to sit this one out—his face a little green. I have a feeling he's reached his cotton candy limit.

Karen gives dad a quick kiss and yells. "You have to watch us up there, Gramps! We're going to be so high!"

He laughs, cupping a hand around his mouth. "Okay, but make sure to wave when you're at the top so I know which ones are you—I won't be able to tell you apart from the clouds!"

Karen and Theresa pile into a car together, giggling with excitement waving wildly to Mom and Dad. Mike and Petey climb into the one behind them. Then Patty and Caroline take the next.

44

As I reach the front of the line, Frank steps up beside me.

"Ladies first," he says, that now-familiar grin tugging at one corner of his mouth.

I slide into the seat, and he follows—folding himself in beside me like it's the most natural thing in the world.

The bar lowers with a *thunk*. The wheel jerks to life, and we start to rise, slow and steady into the sky.

The wheel creaks as we rise higher, the air shifting cooler the farther we get from the crowd. From up here, the boardwalk looks like a patchwork of blinking lights and shadows. I can hear distant music drifting upward, mixed with laughter and a vendor yelling about peanuts to no one in particular—it feels like this should be the soundtrack of the boardwalk, and of the summer, I suppose.

Frank shifts slightly beside me. "I gotta say, you seem remarkably calm for someone dangling this high up with a near-stranger."

I smirk. "You carried my dresser. That makes you slightly less than a stranger."

He nods seriously. "True. Very intimate piece of furniture."

I stifle a laugh. "And you danced with it! A foxtrot if I'm not mistaken."

He chuckles, low and rich. "So, what about you? You seem like the type who'd have rules about Ferris wheel seating. Like, don't sit with a man unless you've seen his résumé."

"Incorrect," I say. "But I do prefer men who can spell résumé."

That gets him—he tips his head back and laughs, an unguarded kind of sound that makes something flutter in my chest.

"Good news then," he says, grinning. "I won the spelling bee in fifth grade. Trophy and everything."

"Impressive," I say. "And what do you do now, Mr. Fifth Grade Champion?"

I work for the paper," he says casually. "*The Daily News*, actually. So I make sure people spell 'résumé' correctly for a living."

My eyebrows shoot up. "The paper? Like the *paper* paper?"

That honeyed laugh rolls out again, curling around me in the warm night air.

"You sound surprised."

"I am. I just didn't expect—well, you're so—I mean…"

"Are you stammering, Miss Trudy?"

"Oh, hush." I swat at him. "I just meant…" I gesture vaguely at his broad shoulders. "You're very strong. And well—look at you."

That makes him smile, then something shifts in it. His laugh softens into something quieter, a little more serious.

"Well," he says, glancing out at the skyline, "I enlisted at eighteen and served in Korea. Got used to the routine. Keeping in shape helps me clear my head. A healthy body, healthy mind." He shrugs like it's nothing.

I nod, a little surprised at the sincerity. "I can see why you and Mike would get along."

He looks at me again, steadier now. "You think I'm all muscle and no words, huh?"

I grin. "Well, not anymore. So, I still reserve judgment until I see that spelling trophy."

A few moments pass in companionable silence as the wheel inches us toward the top. Below, the kids are pointing toward the sky just as the first firework bursts open—gold and loud and bright. It shimmers across the boardwalk, coloring everything for a heartbeat.

I'm surprised how comfortable it feels, just sitting here next to him. No pressure to fill the silence. No need to try.

"Mike's a lucky guy," Frank says suddenly.

It sounds like a thought that slipped out before he could stop it.

"How do you mean?" I ask automatically.

He nods toward the kids squealing in delight and then over to Annette, who's laughing and wiping salt off Denise's cheek with the corner of her shirt. "Family," he says simply, with a note of something wistful.

I turn toward him, watching the light from the fireworks reflect in his eyes. There's something unreadable there— quiet, grounded. A depth I hadn't expected.

"There's a lot more to you than meets the eye, isn't there, Frank?" I say, trying to make it light.

He waggles his eyebrows dramatically. "But what meets the eye is pretty nice, eh?" He throws a theatrical flex of his arm for good measure. Clearly joking, I think he doesn't realize how handsome he is.

That makes me laugh—loud and unguarded.

The kind that bubbles out before you can polish it. The kind that makes you wonder what else this man might surprise you with.

By the time the Ferris wheel slows, the girls are rubbing at tired eyes they're barely able to keep open. It's clear the night's winding down, so the whole group gathers near the exit to say their goodbyes. I walk with Mike, Annette, our parents and the kids back to Mike's car, savoring the last bits of sea breeze and summer.

Annette and I wrestle the stroller into the trunk—a feat that takes far more effort than I'd imagined and sparks way more laughter than Mike bargained for. I heard him call out *what's going on back there* at least twice, but we were too busy doubled over in giggles to reply. Somehow, though, we got it done. Karen hugs me tight. Theresa insists she's not tired but yawns mid-sentence. Michael Jr. offers a wave then hops in the car. Dad kisses each of them on the head and Mom blows them each a kiss as they load into the car, then another once they're in the car. Frank was right about one thing. Mike is lucky, but so am I. This family.... they're mine too, and I love them so deeply. After Mike and Annette drive off, Mom and Dad wrap me in tight hugs, each pressing a kiss to my cheek before heading toward Dad's van for the ride home. They'd offered to drive me, but I craved the hum of the subway and a quiet moment alone, and I didn't want them to go out of their way. I watched them walk to the van, breathing in deeply the salt and popcorn scented air and letting the day go with my breath, holding tight to the good.

Then I'm alone again, the boardwalk quieter now, the carnival lights beginning to dim.

I head toward the Stillwell Avenue subway station. On my way, I make sure to pick up *The Daily News* for the ride.

Chapter 4

"Courage is not the absence of fear, but the triumph over it."
—Nelson Mandela

The halls smell like floor wax, pencil shavings, and crayons. Somewhere down the corridor, a bell rings—sharp, insistent, full of expectation. It's amazing how being immersed in these sounds and smells makes me feel like a child again. I take a deep breath and straighten the collar of my blouse. My new shoes pinch slightly, and I remind myself that confidence is a posture, not a feeling—no matter how loudly my toes protest.

St. Agnes School in Queens is already humming with life. Uniforms swish past me—white socks and navy skirts, boys' ties slightly crooked. The sound of nuns' heels clicking down the hallway echoes like a metronome. I find my classroom tucked down the second-floor corridor, Room 3B, and the plaque outside reads "Miss Kirchberger, third grade." It still doesn't feel real. That's me. This is my room. My belly flip-flops. I'm slowly learning that those first-day jitters don't stop when you graduate.

I grip my lesson plan binder like a lifeline. I stand there for a second, trying to steel my nerves, then catch my reflection in the window and force a small smile. I'm hoping my blond hair reads as bouncy elegance—not Shirley Temple. I meet my own eyes—blue, deep, and wide with nerves I can't quite hide. I analyze my face now—sharp cheekbones, a strong jawline—features that don't quite match the softness of my round face, yet somehow work together.

Deep breaths. This is what I wanted. A classroom of my own. I worked hard for this and I want to prove that I can do this, and do it well. I take a deep breath. *Find three good things.* I have my own classroom. My outfit says *"professional"* even if my shoes say *"regret."* And I managed to keep my coffee down despite a nervous system operating at full Broadway overture. That counts. *There, that's three.* I let out a deep breath. Okay, I can do this.

"Morning, Miss Kirchberger," one of the older nuns says with a nod as she passes. I nod back, trying to hide the fact that my stomach is doing somersaults. I don't know who's more nervous for their first day, me or the kids.

And then: the sound of chairs scraping. Chatter rising. The tiny rumble of thirty third-graders filing in with wide eyes and louder voices.

"Good morning class," I say, brightly and adding as much confidence as I can.

By the end of the day, I'm exhausted. The kids were nervous, but we all made it through the day together, and I feel excited about what the school year will bring.

"So, how'd it go?" asks the teacher next door. I still don't know her name, but I've noticed her a few times—standing just outside the room, stealing glances through the window.

"I think okay. Some hiccups here and there. I couldn't find the chalk for the first twenty minutes, I don't think there's a garbage can in here, and also… how do you get them to *listen* to you?"

She laughs, not unkindly—she clearly has a few years at this under her belt. "Just wait until after Halloween, things tend to settle around then. They'll be locked into the routine and know what to expect—that goes for you too. They'll know what they can get away with." She looks up at me from under her glasses. "So set the tone early, nurture later. Rules first. Of course, that's only my opinion." She adds a smile. I think she does it so she doesn't sound bossy.

My shoulders slump down. "Thank you! I'll take any advice I can get. I'm excited, I just also know I'm new and want to do a good job here. It's not just a job, it's their futures."

It's like I rang a bell and I see her perk up.

"Well, you can always come to me. I'm right next door," she says, pointing to her name placard. *Mrs. DeMarco*, it reads.

"Thanks. I think having a friend here will make all the difference."

"Oh, it's the difference between sinking and swimming," she says, with a conspiratorial smile.

Pretty sure that was a test. And if so? I passed. I think we're going to get along just fine.

I make it through the first week by the skin of my teeth.

I lose the chalk three times. I misspell a word on the blackboard during social studies (I don't *think* they noticed, however one boy definitely squinted suspiciously). The garbage can still doesn't show up by day four, so I fashioned a makeshift one out of a shopping bag I brought from home. It keeps tipping over until one of the girls volunteers to hold it during cleanup. I think that counts as teamwork.

I ask Mrs. DeMarco again for advice on getting the children to listen, and she reminds me to be firm.

Eventually, the children start to listen—not all at once, not consistently, but in small ways. A hush during attendance. A raised hand instead of a shouted answer. A few stay behind to help straighten desks. They're getting there. I'm getting there.

I feel like I deserve a medal. Maybe a parade, with floats and all.

Why they don't hand out awards for surviving your first few weeks of teaching still boggles the mind.

Each evening, I come home more exhausted than the last. My feet ache, my voice is hoarse, and my brain feels like it's been wrung out and hung up to dry. On top of it all, there's this quiet, persistent pride humming underneath it all. I'm doing something that matters. I'm building something, even if it's slow. Even if it's messy.

Sometimes, I sit on the edge of my bed at night with a cup of tea and stare at the wall for a full ten minutes before remembering to breathe. Then I remember one of them said something funny, or drew me a picture, or called me "Miss Churchburger" by accident—and I laugh. And I feel it. That sense of purpose. Of beginning.

And tomorrow, I'll do it all again.

Somewhere in the madness of it all, Henry called to ask what time my lunch usually is.

"Eleven-twenty-five," I told him.

"Very specific," he said.

"Well, what do you expect? It's a school. Everything is very specific and punctual." I laughed.

There was a pause, and then: "There's a little park near the school. Maybe we can meet and eat a packed lunch together?"

"That sounds lovely," I said.

When I get to the park, the bench where he asked me to meet him is easy to spot. It's tucked beneath a patch of bare-limbed trees, their branches rattling gently above like an old song. The paint on the slats has long since chipped away, leaving behind soft splinters and worn grooves from years of use. There's a crooked plaque on the back reads "Donated by the Garden Society of Brooklyn, 1948," though the G has half-faded, making it look like it was gifted by the *arden society*. Which could be a secret club for all I know.

The seat still holds a little warmth from the morning sun. Pigeons coo nearby, pecking at forgotten crumbs. It isn't overly grand or ostentatious, but that's half the charm though—two sandwiches. Two thermoses. A paper napkin with a grease spot shaped like Michigan, or maybe Ohio depending on how you turn it.

We chat easily as my thirty-minute lunch ticks by. And just as I start to gather my things, he asks if I'd like to go to the drive-in with him sometime.

"I need to know a man better before getting in a car with him for two hours," I tease.

He laughs. "Then I'll see you at 11:25 next week."

Those first weeks pass in a blur of construction paper scraps and recess whistles, and before I know it, Saturday evening has arrived—my actual date with Henry. The drive-in.

We've chatted here and there during those weekly lunchtime meetups, but those are quick, light. This? This feels like an actual date.

He picks me up in a brand spankin' new cherry red 1963 Ford Galaxie 500 Convertible. Which, I suppose, is convenient if I need to make a quick getaway. No roof to slow me down. I mentally file the car type away for Patty and Caroline—it's exactly the kind of thing they'd want to know. It's flashier than I'd usually go for, but I can't deny it's beautiful.

The Beach Boys' "Surfin' U.S.A." is playing loud enough to rattle the sidewalk as he pulls up. I laugh, tuck my bag under my arm, and slide into the passenger seat. It smells faintly of leather, cologne, and whatever it is that makes men think a car is a personality trait.

"Hey stranger!" I say "Very subtle." I gesture to the car.

He winks. "Well hello there, Cinnamon Girl. Or should I say, "Teacher Lady?"

"Call me whatever you'd like—as long as you call me," I say, laughing at my own joke.

"Call you mine, you mean?" he shoots back smoothly.

I mock gasp. "Presumptive." I wag my finger at him, scolding like a sitcom housewife.

He just laughs—like he's already proud of getting under my skin.

"And where exactly did this idea that women belong to men come from?" I tease. "Last I checked, my driver's license doesn't say property of so-and-so."

I give a light flick of my hand, like brushing away a silly idea.

"No, but you've got your father's last name, right? And then someday, you'd take your husband's…"

He lets the sentence hang in the air, his grin widening like he knows he's pushing my buttons.

"*If* I get married," I shoot back sweetly, lifting an eyebrow. *There*. That'll show him. I stick out my tongue.

I start to sing along to the radio and he turns it up so he can join in. It's nice.

We drive like that for a while, windows down, the wind threading through my hair. The hum of the tires on the road becomes background music, and for a little while, I let myself forget everything else.

By the time we pull into the drive-in, the sky has shifted to that dusky purple that means the movie's about to start. Henry parks the Ford backwards, so we can sit on the trunk with a blanket draped across it and a paper tray of fries between us. The screen flickers to life as the previews roll—trailers for space adventures and beach party comedies, all louder than they need to be.

He tosses a piece of popcorn into his mouth and stretches back on one arm. "This is perfect, isn't it? The car, the movie, the company…" He nudges my knee lightly with his.

I smile. It *is* nice. The warm breeze, the smell of popcorn and motor oil, the quiet hum of other couples leaning into each other beneath the stars.

"Don't forget the fries," I add, grabbing one dramatically, and weirdly feeling the need to divert attention.

I glance over. He's grinning at me in that charming, perfectly practiced way of his. The kind that would look just as at home in an ad for shaving cream.

The movie starts—something dramatic and sweeping—and we settle in. He puts his arm behind me. Not quite around me, just resting on the edge of the blanket. I don't move away, but I don't lean in either.

He turns to me once during a romantic scene and says, low and casual, "So… what do you think your future husband's doing right now?"

I blink at the screen, then over at him. "Well, if he's smart, he's probably not calling himself my future husband while I'm trying to watch a movie."

Suddenly, someone named *Frankie* is sweeping across the movie screen, and my mind is drifting—to Ferris wheels and fireworks. I feel a tightening in my chest. *Snap out of it, Trudy.*

He laughs—easily, not wounded, and not noticing my wandering mind. "Fair enough."

Henry reaches for more popcorn. I watch the screen, quiet.

It's all very nice. A lovely evening from beginning to end. He doesn't try to kiss me, which I'm quietly grateful for. Maybe he took my "*presumptive*" comment to heart, and that's fine with me.

I like him. I do. It's fun, and our banter is easy.

He drops me off and we make a plan to see each other again. I think that will be nice.

September flies by in a blur.

I'm starting to get the hang of this—lesson plans, attendance sheets, even the lunch line. At least, that's what I thought... until I looked down and realized I was wearing two different shoes. Same style. Two entirely different colors.

I hang my head in my hands.

I've looked like this all day.

I rode the bus like this. Greeted the principal like this.

Well, at least I'm finally making headway with the kids. If they noticed, they didn't say anything. (Small mercies.)

Later that afternoon, I'm sorting through the mail—bills, coupons, catalogues, *The Daily News* (which I've now subscribed to)—when I spot one from an address I don't recognize, with a last name I don't know. *Who on Earth is Mr. Madden?*

I open it.

And you could've knocked me down with a feather.

It's from Frank.

Hi Trudy,
(I hope it's okay that I call you that. "Miss Kirchberger" felt a little too formal for someone I rode a Ferris wheel with.)

I promise this isn't as strange as it seems—I remembered your address from moving day. Not because I'm a creep, just because you labeled your boxes very impressively. (Truly. The handwriting? A+.)

I figured you might be busy conquering your classroom. I've been meaning to write, but didn't want to come off too strong. Still, I'd be kicking myself if I didn't at least say— I really enjoyed talking with you. The kind of talking that sticks in your mind long after it ends. You made a long day feel a lot shorter. And I don't know about you, but people like that don't come around that often from me.

I don't know if you like letters (I'm partial to them), but if you do, and if this one made you smile even a little, maybe you'll write back?

And if not—no pressure. That's your prerogative of course, and I'm just glad I had the chance to say hello.

All the best (and then some),
Frank

P.S. Give the dresser my best.

I must have read it seven times. He's funny. And *charming*. And he wrote me a letter. I don't know what—or how—to feel about it just yet. I *do* know I don't want to just stand here, staring at this letter and rereading it over and over. Which, I've just realized, is exactly what I've been doing for the past several minutes.

I flop down onto the couch and decide to give Patty a call. She'd get a kick out of my life the past few weeks. She's getting ready for night school—nursing classes over at the community college. I picture her brushing her hair into a neat flip with one hand and balancing a cup of Sanka in the other.

"Hello?" she answers on the second ring, a little out of breath.

"It's me," I say. "I know you're busy so I won't be long—I need you to hear about the fashion statement I accidentally made today."

"Oh boy. What happened?"

"I wore two different shoes to school."

A pause. Then a snort. "Please tell me they were two different styles—one flat and one heel."

61

"Same style, different color. One black, one navy. I looked like a walking optical illusion."

She howls. "And this is the woman shaping the minds of tomorrow."

"I know," I groan. "The children deserve better."

"Well," she says, still laughing, "at least you've got that hot date to distract you. How's Mr. Cinnamon Stick?"

"Henry is... nice," I say, stretching out the word like a rubber band. "He took me to the drive-in and didn't talk during the movie, which I feel like should count for something."

Whenever I'm out with him I can't help but think about how I know my parents would adore him—he has a respectable job, he's put together, the whole kit and caboodle. The kind of guy you bring to Sunday dinner and don't have to explain.

"Anyway..." I shift, tucking one leg under me on the couch. "Enough about me. How's school going?"

Patty groans. "My feet hurt, my back hurts, and yesterday I had to give a sponge bath to a man who kept calling me 'sweetheart.' I *did* learn how to take blood pressure without looking like I'm strangling the patient, so I guess that's progress."

"That's absolutely progress!"

"Well, I only nearly passed out once this week, so I'm basically Florence Nightingale."

I laugh. "At this rate, I'll be calling you Nurse Patty by Christmas."

"Let's not get ahead of ourselves," she says with a laugh. "I still can't fold a hospital corner to save my life, and my uniform makes me look like I'm in a school play."

"You'll be the best-looking nurse on the ward. You always had good posture."

"Oh, shut up," she says, though I can hear her smiling. "I should get going, but we should make a plan for me to come visit soon"

"Yes, please."

We hang up and I'm still feeling unsettled. Frank's letter stares at me from the coffee table like it knows something I don't. I pick it up, then put it back down. Then pick it up again.

Of course I want to write him back— I wonder if that would seem too eager? Is there some unwritten rule about how long you're supposed to wait before replying to a boy who sends you a letter?

I already find myself wondering when the next one might come. What if he doesn't write again? What if he does, and it's not as charming as the first? What if it's more charming?

I sigh and fall back against the cushions. Maybe I'll wait a day. Maybe two. But… probably not.

Ten minutes later, I'm at the kitchen table with a pen in hand and half a cup of tea by my elbow. I smooth out the paper, stare at it for a second, then start writing.

Dear Frank,

Thank you for the letter. It was the most unexpected and——if I'm being honest——thoroughly delightful surprise. I haven't received a letter in ages and yours was such a lovely change of pace. And to your point, I wouldn't say you're a creep, more that you have a wonderful memory. I couldn't imagine remembering such a thing when surviving the heat was my primary focus.

I pause, chewing the cap of the pen.

I probably shouldn't be smiling this much while writing.

On a serious note…. I enjoy talking to you too, Frank. So, whenever you'd like to write back, I look forward to reading it.

Sincerely,
Trudy

P.S. I will say, it doesn't bode well for you that after such an intimate dance, it took you nearly a month to ask how the dresser is doing. Shame on you, Frank. She's been beside herself——wondering what she did wrong and how she managed to fall out of favor so quickly. Tisk tisk.

I sit at the table for another hour, grading the spelling tests we gave today, feeling a quiet satisfaction at how well they're doing. A few of them missed one or two of the challenge words—then again, they're challenge words for a reason.

Neighbor and *through* can trip up a third grader pretty easily. Honestly, they trip up a good number of adults, too. Probably not Frank though, working at the paper and all… *focus, Trudy…*

I sigh deeply and stretch back in the chair, my spine giving a small crack of protest. When I glance up at the clock, my eyes suddenly feel heavier. I gather the graded papers into a neat stack, then shuffle off to my room.

Snatching my copy of *Grandmother and the Priests* from the nightstand—a new release I couldn't resist plucking from a bookshop display last week—I slide under the covers and read until the words start to blur.

I wake up to a crisp October morning and decide to call my mom. We haven't connected in a bit, and I find myself missing her.

I make a cup of tea, adding a touch of cinnamon and milk, then wrap my hands around the mug and watch the steam swirl upward, curling into the warmth.

Outside, the city stirs slowly—buses groaning to life, footsteps tapping on the pavement, the faint clatter of someone walking their dog two floors down.

I love mornings like this. A little cool, a little quiet. The world feels like it's on the precipice—a tipping point, teetering into something new.

I pick up the receiver and stick my finger into the first number, dragging it around the dial until it clicks back into place. One by one—click, whir, pause—I work my way through the rest. There's something oddly satisfying about it, like the phone is thinking right along with me.

My mother answers on the fourth ring and I feel my throat tightening—I've missed her more than I'd realized.

I clear my throat. "Hi Mom"

"Ah! My Trud-a-la, I was wondering when you would call. I've been wanting to talk to you but didn't want to push and let you settle into your space, you know"

I laugh. "Of course, would you like to hear how it's all going?"

"Is that a real question, my dear? Of course! Start from the very beginning! Don't leave out a thing."

We chat for nearly two and a half hours, my dad chiming in every so often. He found a new and interesting coin in one of the vending machines, Theresa did a cartwheel, Karen drew him a beautiful picture, and he's been bringing toys to all the kids on their block. It started out with just the grandkids but its grown—and he has no intentions of stopping it. He thinks it's hysterical how they come running when they see his van pull up. "It's like a beacon," he laughs. "That white van might as well have sirens and confetti." From somewhere in the background, I hear Mom call out, "My apple fritters may as well be chopped liver!"

Then the undertone of concern, he wants to know how I am, if the neighborhood really does feel safe.

I tell them how school's been going—about my shoe mishap, and how I got in a bit of trouble for bringing hot tea into my classroom.

"It's not a café, Miss Kirchberger," I mimic, putting on my prissiest voice.

I mention my dates with Henry, and the letters with Frank.

By the time we hang up, I feel better. Lighter. Content.

I get dressed and head down to the deli on the corner—I'm running low on coffee and tea, and while I'm out, I figure I'll mail that letter. There's a public mailbox just outside, standing there like it's waiting for me, its blue mouth gaping open.

I hover for a moment. *This is ridiculous. Just drop it in!*

I slide the letter through the slot—much more gently than necessary—and feel a rush of nerves almost instantly. And with it, a flurry of anticipation.

I don't want to admit how badly I want him to write to me again.

I'm not proud to admit, I check the mail every day, like a child ruffling through their Christmas stockings, digging to find a treasure. By Wednesday, I strike gold—Frank had written me back. I cannot stop the smile that has taken over my face, and my greedy hands tear it open before I can stop them.

Dear Trudy,

I'm relieved to know my letter didn't land in the category of "questionable mail." I worried it might've been too forward, or worse, one of those strange coupons people never remember signing up for.

You've made my day (possibly my whole week) by writing back.

For the record, I maintain that I'm only creepy on Tuesdays, and even then, only before noon—so hopefully the letter doesn't reach you within that window. The rest

68

of the time, I just happen to recall certain things. Like how the heat that day made your freckles stand out. How you had this very specific look when you took charge of the situation. How you make a mean glass of lemonade.

But more than anything: the sound of your laugh—high in the clouds, mixed with the booming of fireworks.
Beautiful.

Also: noted. A month is too long. Please give the dresser my sincerest apologies. I didn't mean to ignore her—I just assumed she needed time to recover. (I did too.) But now that you've opened the door, I'm afraid she—and you—may be hearing from me a lot more often.

Though between us, I should probably admit... I've got my eye on someone new these days. Don't tell her, though. Wouldn't want to break her heart if it turns out it's one-sided.

Write again soon—if you feel like it.

Yours (not quite creepily),
Frank

I blink and cover my smiling mouth. My goodness. What an absolute delight this man is. I feel a giddiness bubbling up in me that I haven't felt since I was a child. I was right, this man is pure charm, and something else—something I can't quite put my finger on, but heaven knows I'd like to.

I feel very little shame in the fact that I sit down to immediately write a reply.

Dear Frank,

Well, congratulations. You've officially made me laugh out loud alone in my kitchen like a lunatic. I hope you're pleased with yourself. I nearly spilled tea down my blouse.

(And for the record, if you are creepy on Tuesdays, I'm willing to make an exception. And lucky for you, your letter arrived on a Wednesday.)

I won't lie: I've reread the part about the fireworks three times. Maybe four. It was a good night, wasn't it? I do think I probably laughed louder than the fireworks, and that's saying something. Is it more about how funny you are or how loud I am? No way to know, I guess. Unless, we see each other again and there happen to be fireworks.

(Also, you've officially made my dresser blush. She's still recovering but accepts your apology.)

As for this "someone new" you've got your eye on——I'm sure she's very lucky. If she knows what's good for her, she'll write you back. Quickly. I'd love to hear more about her.

Yours in curiosity,
Trudy

I look down at the letter that just so easily poured out of my pen, the ink moving like magic across my page. It was so instinctive, like he was sitting across the table from me. The room felt less empty while I was writing, and now that I'd finished, less so.

I set the letter aside, smoothing the page once before folding it gently and sliding it into an envelope. I don't seal it just yet—I like the idea of it sitting nearby a little longer, like company I'm not quite ready to see out.

I glance at the stack of papers waiting for me on the table. Social studies quizzes. I pull out Teddy's—such a funny boy, always making me laugh, even when he's supposed to be serious.

Q: What do we call the leader of our country?
"Boss of America."
I chuckle. *I'll let President Kennedy know he's been promoted.*

Q: Why do we celebrate Independence Day?
"Because George Washington liked fireworks."
I sigh. *Teddy.*

Q: What is a map used for?
"To find buried treasure at Grandma's house."
I laugh outright at this one. He's always bringing in the most random things in his pockets. Once, it was a hard-boiled egg. Another time, an acorn. When I asked him why, he whispered something about treasures. That explains *that.*

Q: What does a community need to work well together?
"Cookies. And not yelling."

I pick up my red pen. It gives my hands something to do while my thoughts refuse to quiet.

I still feel a little like he's in the room—and I'm realizing how much I like that feeling.

Chapter 5

"When black cats prowl and pumpkins gleam, may luck be yours on Halloween!" — Unknown

Wednesday comes, and with it my weekly lunch date with Henry.

There's a definite chill in the air now, so I remember to wear a warmer coat and a sweater. He's in one of those long, trench-style coats, hands tucked into the deep pockets like he's settling in for a while. We chat easily at our little bench. Tomorrow is Halloween, and I ask if he has any plans.

"Of course not—well, aside from handing out candy to kids that come by," he says. "Why? Are you planning on dressing up?" he adds with a mockingly raised brow.

"I'll have a full day with the kids, I'm sure. Then handing out candy in the evening... maybe I'll sneak a few for myself." I'm not certain why, but I feel defensive. I shouldn't care what he thinks. And yet, I do, just enough to feel a little foolish.

I add, "I might dress up as a cat and prowl around looking for candy."

He lets out a sharp laugh. "You're joking, of course. You're a grown woman. You can't possibly be thinking of wearing a costume."

I bristle, just slightly, but keep my tone light. "Well, I'm going to do a little something for the children. And how else am I supposed to get candy?" I say, letting the words drip with faux sweetness.

He laughs again, louder this time. "I'll make sure to save you a Kit Kat for next week," he says with a wink.

I smile but glance at my watch. I have to cut lunch short today—I've got to squeeze in as much as I can before tomorrow so I can make time for a small Halloween party at school. He kisses my cheek, and I'm a little surprised— but I don't pull away.

"Until next week," he says.

I smile again, but something inside me pulls back. It was just a comment, a silly comment, but it sticks.

Why is it so hard to let people have a little joy?

My head spins as I walk inside. I like Henry. He's nice. Charming, even. But there's something about him— something I can't quite name—that makes me wonder if this is really worth continuing.

It's easy. He's easy. Fun enough to pass the time.

But, every so often, something slips through—a tone, a glance, a comment—and the hairs on the back of my neck stand up in warning. Perhaps I'm being overly sensitive. Or perhaps I've just spent too long pretending not to notice things that make me feel small. It's hard to tell where instinct ends and insecurity begins.

Either way, I need to focus on the children waiting for me at their desks, so I tuck the feeling away, unsure what to make of it.

I walk in quickly and jump right into our lesson. I want to make sure we stay on track today so they'll have time to enjoy the craziness of tomorrow. I'm fully aware their minds are on costumes and possible candy hauls, not social studies—but I'm moving around like a dancing circus monkey, doing everything short of juggling apples just to keep their attention.

"All right class," I say, tapping the chalkboard with my pointer stick like I'm conducting a very tiny orchestra, "who remembers how we start the song?"

A few hands shoot up. A few groans follow. And then from the front row, Teddy belts out the first line with zero warning:

"America's president number one: Founding Father Washington."

Laughter ripples through the room, then others join in, bouncing in their seats as they sing our presidential roll call, slightly off-key yet full of gusto.

"John Adams, second president: the very first White House resident."

We make it all the way to Andrew Jackson before things start to fall apart. I let them stumble a little—some confusion between Polk and Pierce—before gently guiding them back on track. When we hit Abraham Lincoln, I mime a tall hat, and someone in the back yells, "Miss Kirchberger, you're really good at that."

"I'll take that as a compliment," I say, adjusting my imaginary stovepipe. "Alright, let's talk Washington. Who remembers something about him?"

Kathy's hand shoots up before I've even finished the question.

"He had wooden teeth!" she announces proudly.

"Well," I say, drawing out the word, "that's what people used to think. Actually, his dentures were made of ivory, metal… and even horse teeth."

A collective groan echoes across the room.

"That's *disgusting*," Teddy says.

"Did they fall out when he sneezed?" Jimmy asks, very seriously.

"I don't know," I reply, "but I hope not. I imagine he kept his mouth shut on windy days."

Richard squints. "Where's the cherry tree now?"

"What cherry tree?"

"The one he chopped down."

I try not to laugh. "That story was made up to show how honest he was. He probably never chopped down a cherry tree at all."

Linda gasps. "So… George Washington lied about not lying?"

"Not exactly," I say. "Someone else made it up for him."

She folds her arms, unconvinced. "History is very suspicious."

"I agree."

Then Heather raises her hand, her voice quieter than the others. "Miss Kirchberger… which president would you be?"

The room stills, all of them watching me.

I smile. "I think I'd be Eleanor Roosevelt. She wasn't president herself—nonetheless, she led in so many ways. She stood up for people, spoke out for what was right, and she didn't let anyone tell her she couldn't make a difference."

They're quiet for a second. Then Donna tilts her head. "Was she the one with the really good hats?"

"She was."

"Cool," she says, nodding.

Teddy raises his hand and wiggles in his chair. "Which one is my president?"

I blink. "Excuse me?"

"My name's Teddy. So, who's the Teddy president?"

I grin. "Ah, Theodore Roosevelt. Number twenty-six. A very bold president—he liked hiking and wrestling and giving long speeches."

"Did he invent me?" Teddy asks.

"Close. A toy company made the first 'teddy bear' after he refused to shoot a bear cub on a hunting trip. They named it in his honor."

Teddy beams. "I knew I was important."

I laugh. "Very. And if you ever become president, I expect a statue in the classroom."

We make it through the end of the day and, somehow— defying all odds—Halloween too.

By the time I close the classroom door and switch off the lights, I feel like I've been run over by a parade float. Halloween plus third graders is not for the faint of heart.

My cat ears are drooping slightly to one side—I didn't realize they'd been lopsided since lunch.

The party only lasted twenty-five minutes, and somehow the room still looked like it had hosted a full-scale alien invasion. I brought homemade cupcakes—well I took them out of the box from the bakery. That counts in my book.

The kids still had to wear their uniforms, but were allowed to wear a bit of orange over it. So the room looked like the inside of a pumpkin for most of the day.

One girl, Kathy, gave me a drawing of a black cat standing on two legs, teaching math. She labeled it "Miss Kirch*pur*ger." I tucked it into my bag like a piece of fine art worthy of a spot in the Met. *Clever girl.*

Now, the building is quiet. My feet ache, my voice is gone, and I can't tell if I'm more sugar-rushed or sugar-crashed.

Still, I smile. They had fun.

And tomorrow, we'll go back to long division and spelling lists.

For today though, they're just kids. And I'm just a very tired cat.

As I'm leaving the school, I remember that last week, a slightly less exhausted version of me called Patty and Caroline to meet for coffee after school. Miraculously, we found a time and place that worked for all three of us, though it felt like trying to pull a car down the street with a rope. However exhausted I may be, I still need to see them, even if just briefly. Our schedules have all been a bit chaotic lately, and getting a moment of time with people like this always makes me feel lighter.

I find Patty and Caroline already waiting in a cozy booth. Patty's brown hair is pulled neatly away from her face, her nurse's cap still pinned in place, the uniform still on. She looks so professional, the dress and apron a pristine, almost glowing white. Today however, there's a small felt pumpkin pinned to her chest. It sticks out like a sore thumb.

Caroline, on the other hand, is all fall color and confidence. She's in a deep orange blouse that makes her auburn hair look like it was painted to match. She has on a sleek pencil skirt, silk scarf, and a pumpkin-themed headband that should be too much—and yet, on her, it just works.

I see they've already ordered me a tea and are talking grandly, hands flying and voices low with intrigue. I make my way over and slide into the booth. We chat, about everything and nothing all at once.

Then something shifts. It's time for the real stuff.

I start, mostly because I practically plopped my whole body into the seat, my work bag making a very noisy *thunk* as I sat. It feels overly dramatic—it also seems like the perfect opener to unload the things that have been sitting on my chest.

"I love teaching, I really do. I… I just don't want to fail at this. Every day I look out at those kids, and their big eyes look back at me like I'm supposed to have all the answers. Like I have to be perfect."

"No one needs you to be perfect, Trudy," Caroline says softly.

"But I feel like I should be—for them. I think about how I'd want my nieces and nephew to feel with their teacher. Safe. Heard. Inspired, even. To learn something new every single day. I want to be that for all of them. And yet most days I feel like I've been tossed into the deep sea without swimming lessons. Or a life jacket. I'd settle for one of those sad inflatable floaties from the boardwalk."

I pause, then add, "Well, I do have one—Mrs. DeMarco. She's been a pseudo-mentor, and that's helped a lot. When I'm really drowning, she offers a hand. I just hate that I keep needing one. I think I'm doing okay at this. But I don't want to be okay. I want to be... *wonderful*."

"Now who put those expectations on you, darling?" Caroline asks with a smirk.

"Society!" I say, dramatically lifting my hands.

Patty chuckles. "If anything, society wants you to be mediocre. Not to stand out, not to be too loud or too... *good* at anything. Just stay perfectly in the middle."

"Well, yes and no," I counter. "We have to be perfect— but quiet. I think it's not mediocrity society wants. It's unattainable perfection, wrapped in agreeability, with absolutely no visible signs of struggle."

"And do it all in heels!" Caroline adds, raising her mug like a toast.

We laugh.

Patty reaches across the table. "Either way, Trudy—you're just starting. I'm not eight and in your class, so I can't say for certain, but I do know how much you care. And I think that already proves how wonderfully you're doing. Let Mrs. DeMarco help you. We're not all meant to know everything. Don't blame yourself for things you haven't learned yet. You wouldn't fail a student for a lesson they hadn't been taught, right? So why don't you give yourself the same grace?"

I smile and feel a bit of the weight lift from my chest—like they both took it off me themselves.

I glance at Patty. "So... what brought on this new philosophy about mediocrity?"

The sigh that escapes her is so deep, I can tell she's been holding it in for weeks.

"Medicine," she says. "It's such a boys' club."

Caroline and I sit back and let her unload—me with my tea, her with her hot chocolate piled high with an absurd amount of whipped cream.

"I'm about to say something that's going to make me sound like my head is so full of hot air I might as well be a balloon floating over Fifth Avenue," she starts. "But I *know* I'm extraordinary. I *know* I'm doing brilliant work—and yes, I'm still a student. But I'm doing *real* work. *Good* work. And the doctors keep taking credit for it."

She pauses, eyes flashing. "It's just... so disheartening. I'm not asking for a gold star or a parade. But watching someone take credit for something you figured out? It infuriates me.

'You're a nurse, not a doctor.'

'Know your place.'

'You're still learning.'

Blah, blah, blah."

She lets out another frustrated breath, then leans back in her chair, as if the act of saying it aloud has taken something out of her.

"It just gets under my skin," she finishes, quieter now. "Like I'm supposed to keep pretending I don't see it."

Caroline nods slowly. "I get it," she says. "Different corner of the world, same circus."

She stirs the whipped cream into her drink without looking up. "My boss pats my shoulder every time he walks past me. Tells me I type *beautifully*. Once told me I should enter a swimsuit contest because I'd win with just my smile."

She finally looks at us, the corners of her mouth tight. "I'm not trying to cure anyone, but I *am* trying to make a living. And sometimes I still feel like all I'm selling is legs and a laugh."

Patty reaches across and touches her hand. Caroline lets it stay for a moment.

Then she lifts her mug and smirks. "But if I win that swimsuit contest, I am buying us all dinner. And let's be honest, we all *know* I'd win."

"Oh, no question about it," I laugh.

Caroline grins. "Speaking of great legs—you're coming to the Halloween party tomorrow, right? Costumes are mandatory. Obviously."

"Obviously," I say, though I'm already wondering if I'll actually go. I'm so exhausted—but this time with them has invigorated me. I could use some frivolous fun.

"You can bring tall, dark, and perfectly nice, if you want."

"No, that's okay." I shrug. "He seemed to think the idea of dressing up was akin to a child running a business meeting."

"Oh." Caroline glances at Patty, and something wordless passes between them.

"What?"

"Nothing, darling," she says with a too-innocent smile. "I *do* hope you'll dress up as ridiculously as you can."

I point to my cat ears, that have somehow managed to stay on. "I'm sure these will make a second appearance."

Caroline raises her mug. "Well, *meow*."

I glance out the café window as the sun begins to dip, casting everything in gold. None of us say much as we gather our things, but I can feel it in the air—that strange alchemy of laughter and truth, of knowing you're not alone in the battle to be more than what the world expects. It's not everything. Sometimes, it's all you need.

By the time I'm home, I'm exhausted—yet still relatively excited about handing out candy.

Mostly, though, I'm looking forward to putting my feet up and finally starting *The Feminine Mystique*.

I curl up in my chair, still in my school clothes, cat ears resting on the armrest. The buzz of trick-or-treaters fades with the evening. As I flip the page, I find myself rereading the same paragraph twice—thinking instead about Caroline's ridiculous swimsuit comment and everything she has to put up with each day, about how Patty must feel never being acknowledged for her hard work, about how good it felt to say things out loud and not feel wrong for doing it.

The party's tomorrow night.

I'm still not sure I'll go.

I leave the cat ears where I can see them just in case.

The next night, the party is already in full swing by the time I arrive—music spilling out of Caroline's apartment windows, a faint scent of popcorn and something smoky hanging in the air. A group of people are smoking on the steps, one of them dressed as a pirate, another with a construction helmet.

I adjust the black ribbon holding my makeshift cat ears in place and feel a flicker of excitement. It's nice, for once, to mingle with adults instead of third graders. I've gone all in: tail, painted-on nose and whiskers, dressed head-to-toe in black. Caroline was right. If I'm going to dress up, I might as well enjoy it.

So much of my time is spent in a world of children. Tonight feels like a small rebellion, a reminder that I exist outside the classroom. And maybe, at the same time, a reminder to keep playing. To still see the fun the way the kids do.

It's warm and crowded, the lights low, orange bulbs strung along the ceiling like carnival lights. People I sort of know—Caroline's friends from work, a friend of a friend I always forget the name of—float around in bits of costume and conversation. A witch in heels offers me a drink. I take it, more for something to hold than anything else. It's cold in my already cold hands.

I turn, and there he is.

Frank.

My stomach flips. A flush of nerves and something like joy rushes in all at once. I feel a smile tug at the corners of my mouth before I can stop it.

What is he doing here? He seems to be hanging around this group more lately—and I think I like it.

He's just as striking as I remember—maybe more so. A button-down shirt, slacks, a paper cup with a pumpkin on it in one hand, and a bag of candy in the other, like he wandered in from an entirely different kind of party.

And suddenly, we're together. Talking.

"No costume? Caroline was very clear about the rules."

He points to a small plastic badge pinned to his shirt that says SHERIFF.

I laugh, despite myself. "Well, Sheriff, welcome to the chaos."

"And you're a cat?"

"I'm partial to them. One of my students called me Miss Kirch*purr*ger yesterday." I laugh.

He smiles. "Very clever. It's a good look."

I nod toward his candy bag. "Looks like you've got your priorities in order."

"Well, I would've found you first," he says, "but I didn't know you were coming."

I smile. "Aren't you a charmer."

He shrugs, then looks down—just for a second—before lifting his eyes to mine.

"I love your letters," he says quietly. "They're the best part of my week."

We'd been sending them regularly, and still—I look forward to each one like a child waiting for Santa on Christmas Eve.

I feel the air leave my lungs.

I'm caught completely off guard. I can't believe he said that—just outright, like that. I blink at him a few times, then glance down, flustered.

"Me too," I say softly.

Then again, firmer: "Me too. You're so brilliant, and funny, and... I'm really glad you decided to write me."

I lean just a little closer.

And right then, at exactly that second, we both get hit with a spray of water from someone whipping their head back after bobbing for apples.

We freeze. Then look at each other—and burst out laughing.

"Let's go sit," he nods towards the couch and turns to walk towards it, grabbing my hand to help weave me through the crowd.

I follow him, trying not to admit the flutter in my chest at the contact.

But it's there.

It's definitely there.

We sit, and after a minute he subtly drapes his arm around me—like he's just getting more comfortable. Either way, I'm not complaining.

And there we stay. For the rest of the evening.

We talk about everything.

I tell him about school—how yesterday, Teddy stuck a cupcake to his forehead and called himself a unicorn, and how I had to pretend to scold him, even though I thought it was absolutely hilarious.

I tell him about the stray cat I've been leaving milk out for on my balcony, about Kathy and her clever drawings, and about my casual dates with Henry—nothing serious, just... company.

Then I tell him how close I am with Mike and Annette. I describe each of my nieces and nephew so he can picture them too—Michael Jr, brilliant and thoughtful; Karen, with the biggest heart I've ever witnessed in a person, child or adult; Theresa, pint-sized and fearless; and baby Denise, who somehow brings the whole room together with just those big blue eyes of hers.

I tell him about my last phone call with my parents, and how it made me feel a way I didn't quite expect. My mother, who loves to sing and bake. And my father, who lives to make children laugh—and who tries to protect me, sometimes to his own detriment.

He listens—really listens.

Then he talks.

About his time in the war. About how it makes him see injustices everywhere, how he started noticing things he never had before. The way we walk past homeless men like they're furniture. The way people talk down to women like it's a reflex. The things people carry that no one sees.

About his estrangement from his family and what that's done to his soul. How much he secretly misses them, even if he doesn't say it out loud most days. He tells me he has a sister who moved to California. They write to each other, though—not often, but enough to know they still matter.

Time seems to warp around us—soft, slow, weightless. At some point, the music fades and the chatter dies down.

The room is mostly empty.

"Oh," I say, blinking up at him, surprised—almost like waking from a dream. "I guess the party's over."

"Best one I've been to in a long time," Frank says, earnest and quiet.

"Me too."

He leans in, just enough to send a shiver down my spine, and whispers into my ear: "I look forward to your next letter."

He pulls back, close enough that we're sharing the same air.

I feel my heartbeat stutter in my chest.

"As do I," I manage to say, just above a whisper.

Then—he lifts my hand and presses a kiss to the back of it. And he holds my gaze like it's a secret.

I. Melt.

He turns and walks away, leaving me standing there like a popsicle in the summer sun.

I fan myself lightly. *Isn't it October?*

Because suddenly, it feels like I'm melting in the middle of a summer heatwave.

I could still feel the echo of his voice in my ear. But the week continues its arduous task of moving forward, even though something in me feels like it's been tipped gently off its axis.

It's Sunday, and there are letters to send—my own kind of steady heartbeat.

The last Sunday of the month had become a sort of ritual.

I spread my papers across the kitchen table—magazines, envelopes, rubber-banded stacks of receipts. A mug with a cute cat winking, filled with now-lukewarm tea, sat on a coaster. Somewhere down the hall, a Billie Holiday record crackled softly.

I flip open my little spiral ledger. *Donations.*

I run my finger down the page: *Catholic Worker*, $1. *The Ladder*—subscription renewed last week, but I'd tuck in a dollar anyway.

I run my finger further down the page: *ASPCA*, $1. For the little ones without a voice—like my stray cat, currently outside lapping up the milk I've left out.

I like the feeling of it. Sending something out into the world. A small rebellion in the form of a stamp. Not loud and in everyone's face, but a quiet way of helping those I feel need it.

My fingers hesitate at *The Nation* renewal form. I could let that one go this month.

I'd tear out the article about women's wages and take it to Patty anyway. It's something she should definitely read—I think she'll enjoy it.

I fold the single into a plain white envelope and write simply: *Catholic Worker, New York, NY.*

No return address. They don't need to know who it's from—just knowing they'll receive it is enough. It wasn't marching or shouting. Not changing the world in big, bold letters.

But it's *something.*

It's *mine.*

Mike and I like to debate my little quiet contributions.

"People don't need handouts," he chides.

"I just like making sure everyone gets a chance at an equal playing field. It's not fair to expect someone who's homeless to show up with the same expectations as someone who grew up middle class. How do you expect everyone to reach the same finish line when people have different starting lines? This just puts everyone at least closer to a similar start."

"You're enabling people not to work hard."

"I disagree. I'm giving them a leg up so they can show how hard they can work."

"You're throwing away your hard-earned money."

"It's *my* money to throw away, isn't it?"

I stick out my tongue, and on we go.
He loves to debate—for debating's sake.

I lick the final envelope, smooth it with my palm, and lean back in my chair.

No one will know except me.

But isn't that enough?

Chapter 6

"A man may die, nations may rise and fall, but an idea lives on." — *John F. Kennedy*

Wednesday comes and with it another lunch date with Henry at our little bench. The wind has a bite to it this afternoon, sharper than I expected. I pull my coat tighter as I spot Henry already waiting on the bench, hands tucked in his pockets, posture straight yet still relaxed. He stands when he sees me, and for a moment I think he might say something sweet or charming—instead, he holds out a scarf.

"For you," he says. "Figured you might be cold."

It's pink. Very pink. A soft, rosy shade that clashes slightly with my navy coat—but the way he's looking at me, hopeful and just a little proud, makes me smile anyway. Maybe I *was* being overly sensitive last time I saw him.

"Thank you," I say, looping it around my neck. "Very thoughtful."

He sits beside me, just close enough that our coats brush. "You should've seen the kids on my block," he says. "Absolute mayhem. I thought I had enough candy, but by six o'clock I was down to handing out stray Smarties and a couple of broken lollipops I found at the bottom of the bowl."

I laugh. "You didn't just do pennies at that point?"

"Nope, I'm not a monster."

We settle into an easy rhythm—stories of trick-or-treaters with costumes held together by hope and safety pins, the ones bold enough to come back twice with pillowcases flipped inside out.

The wind picks up and I tug the scarf tighter. It's still not my color, but it's warm, and he's watching me like he's glad I wore it anyway.

"Maybe next year I'll help you hand out candy," he says. "We can be those people—the good house with the full-size bars."

"Big dreams," I laugh, but my voice softens. It's a simple lunch together, nothing grand, there's a quiet kind of care in it though. And I find it sweet. I glance at my watch. Our little half-hour is up.

"Thank you for the scarf," I say with a warm smile.

"You're welcome. Pink is your color, huh?"

I don't correct him. I just smile, wrap my arms around him for a quick hug, and start to turn back toward the school.

He gently grabs my arm before I can take a full step.

"Let's get dinner this weekend."

I hesitate—just for a second, hopefully not enough for him to notice—then nod, my voice soft. "Okay."

He smiles. I offer one more polite glance over my shoulder before slipping back inside.

When I get home there's a letter waiting for me in my mailbox.

November 1, 1963

Dear Trudy,

I hope this finds you warm and dry and not still soaked from rogue apple water. I don't think I've laughed that hard in a while.

I wasn't planning on going to that party. I almost talked myself out of it, actually. I wasn't feeling very festive—I've been a bit tired lately—but I heard there would be candy and the possibility of some good company. I don't know what was sweeter.

Sitting next to you on that couch felt like the first time I exhaled in a long time. You talk about your life with such color—like it matters. And it does, I realize. I felt like I'd known your nieces and nephew by the time you finished the sentence about Denise's big blue eyes. I remember

Theresa too, she talked me into going on the carousel. I was dizzy for an hour.

Your students sound like troublemakers in the best possible way. If Kathy ever publishes a comic strip starring Miss Kirchpurrger, I expect a copy in the mail— maybe I'll add a section into *The Daily*.

Thank you for telling me about your family, too. I know that's not always simple. Families can be... complicated. You listen in a way that makes people want to keep talking. That's rare.

Also, tell me more about Henry. He sounds awful. (Not really, but I'll pretend he is.)

Looking forward to your next letter. And if you see the cat, give him an extra bit of milk for me.

Yours (until someone realizes this badge is a fake),
Sheriff Frank

He called me *his*. And he wrote this the *very next day*. I don't even try to deny how much I love both of those things.

So I settle in to write him back, curling up with my tea and letting the quiet wrap around me. I reread his letter one more time, grinning like a fool, then pull out my favorite pen—the one with the smooth ink—and start writing.

Dear Sheriff Madden,

The badge may be fake, but your timing is suspiciously perfect. The letter arrived just as I sat down with a cup of tea and the last cupcake from the party (of course I saved one for myself). I hope the jury's still out on which was sweeter.

I still can't believe you remembered all the kids' names. I might have to start quizzing you. I've gotten very good at grading. And yes—Theresa does have a way of talking people into things.

I told Kathy you want rights to her Miss Kirchpurrger comic strip. She said only if you draw a sheriff sidekick. I told her I'd see what I could do. She'll want all the royalties I'm sure, as I said, she's very clever.

It meant a lot to me that you listened the way you did. I find it very easy to talk to you, and just as easy to listen.

As for Henry: he's perfectly fine and terribly nice. Which is all very . . . . nice. He doesn't write me letters, anyway.

Tell me more about your sister sometime. And your newspaper. And how you managed to make a couch in a noisy room feel like the quietest place in the world.

I've saved you some candy, by the way. Sheriff's honor.

Yours (unless that badge comes with rules about emotional entanglements),
Trudy

The weekend arrives, and with it, my date with Henry. I was still reeling from Frank's letter—its warmth, its humor, the way he so effortlessly saw me—but I'd told Henry I would go, and he'd seemed genuinely excited the last time we talked. I didn't want to disappoint him. Still, part of me couldn't help but feel like I was stepping into the evening with one foot still rooted in that letter, in a conversation that hadn't yet ended.

He said he was taking me to Delmonico's. I've never been, all I know is that it's upscale—the kind of place you hear about in whispers and see in films, with white tablecloths and menus that don't list prices.

I spend longer than I should getting ready. I try on three dresses before settling on the navy one with the nipped-in waist and the soft satin bow in the back. It's modest yet still elegant, and I pair it with a string of pearls and a coat that doesn't quite match but will have to do. I swipe on a little lipstick—not too much—and fuss with my hair until the curls hold just enough.

By the time I step out the door, I'm not nervous, exactly. I'm aware of myself in a way I haven't been in a while. Not uncomfortable… just self-conscious.

The waiter pulls out my chair like I'm some kind of royalty, and I catch myself suppressing a laugh. Not because it isn't lovely—it is. The chandeliers alone look like they have their own trust fund. Either way, this is all a bit unexpected. And a bit much, if I'm honest.

"Wow," I say, taking in the crisp linens, polished silver. "Are we celebrating something?"

Henry chuckles, brushing off his blazer as he sits across from me. "I just thought we deserved a nice evening."

"A *very* nice evening," I say, raising an eyebrow. "I can change forks every 15 minutes."

He smiles, but doesn't laugh this time. "Well, these are the kinds of things I can do for you."

That quiet little line hangs between us for a beat longer than I expect.

I reach for my water glass, mostly to do something with my hands. "You know I'd have been happy with a slice and a walk through the park."

"I know," he says, looking at me like that's the exact reason he didn't do something simple.

What kind of world are we living in now?

And how will I explain any of this to eight-year-olds on Monday? Hell, how do I make any sense of it myself?

I call my parents, just to hear their voices. Then Mike. I try to call both Caroline and Patty but they don't answer.

Then I call Frank. I just... need to hear his voice.

By the time I hang up, things aren't better—but I can manage until tomorrow.

I'm just on my way to make some tea when the phone rings again. It's Henry. He's worried. We talk for a bit about the state of the world, about how fragile it all suddenly feels.

Monday is declared a national day of mourning, and schools are closed. I spend the day in my apartment, watching as JFK is laid to rest, tears slipping quietly down my cheeks.

I can't take my eyes off Jackie.

So composed. So still. Standing by her husband until the very end, never leaving his side. She walks next to the casket during the funeral procession. I can feel how the weight of that act means something to her. Their last walk together. She handles it all with such grace.

There's something about that—something that lodges in my chest and won't leave.

It sticks with me.

It haunts me.

When Tuesday comes, all those little eyes are looking up at me.

The "whys" and "what nows" are questions I can't fully answer.

I lead them in a prayer and tell them it's okay to feel sad.

This is a sad thing that's happened.

Then, we move on to multiplication.

When I get home, I'm emotionally spent. I sigh deeply and sit on my couch feeling the weight of so much.

Tomorrow, thankfully, is a half day—and then we're off for Thanksgiving break. I'll be heading to Long Island to spend the holiday with Mike, Annette, and the kids. Mom and Dad will be coming too, and I find myself looking forward to it more than I usually do.

I ache for normalcy. For the chaos. For family.

I still need to decide what to bring. There's a bakery nearby—I can stop there tomorrow after school and pick up a pumpkin pie on my way home. That'll be nice.

Speaking of nice, I should probably call Henry and cancel our lunch date this week. With everything going on, I just won't have the time.

When I call, he's more annoyed than I expect that I have to cancel. I didn't mean to disappoint him—but I don't think I have the energy to carry his disappointment too. I feel so guilty that I backtrack, pretending I'd gotten mixed up, and say I actually can make lunch. We compromise on dinner instead, leaving me time to run my errands. He's relieved, but he's still a bit icy.

After the weight of the day, and the coldness from Henry, I decided to sit and write to Frank.

Frank,

Everything has been... heavy. The kind of heavy that sinks into your bones.

I keep going over things, when I dismissed the class early, and then the city seemed to go quiet. Like everyone was holding their breath at the same time. Walter Cronkite's voice breaking was the sound that finally broke me too. I can't get the image of Jackie out of my mind. There's an ache that settled into me after watching her that just won't ebb. Not yet at least, maybe not for a while.

I called my parents. I called Mike.

I called you. Thank you for answering. Your voice settled me more than you know.

You have this way of making things feel less harsh. I kept wishing you were here. Not to fix it——no one can——but just to sit on the couch again and talk about nothing and everything until the world feels a little less cruel.

I called Henry. I tried to cancel our lunch. He didn't take it well, so I backed out... and somehow got roped into dinner instead. I guess I didn't have the energy to explain that grief doesn't work on a schedule.

I'm heading to Long Island Thursday. I'll bring pie. The kids will be loud. And I think that's exactly what I need. A little noise. A little normal. What do you normally do for Thanksgiving?

Don't forget to write——if you'd like. I'd love for you to tell me about your day. Or tell me about the cat you saw once on your paper route that looked like it ran a gambling ring. I could use a story like that right now.

Yours,
Trudy

It's the Wednesday before Thanksgiving, and the air feels heavier than usual. Maybe it's the grief that's still clinging to the city like soot, or maybe it's just me, still shaken from Friday. Henry said he had something "low-key" in mind— just dinner, nothing fancy. He thought it might be a nice distraction. I agreed.

I wear a simple navy dress and a bit of lipstick, hoping to look composed even though I still don't quite feel it.

When I arrive at the restaurant, Henry stands to greet me, all charm and cufflinks. But then I see them—two people rising from the booth behind him.

"Trudy," he says, too brightly, "I want you to meet my parents."

Oh. Did he just say... parents? Maybe they're in town for Thanksgiving and he wants to be polite. That has to be it... right?

I smile on instinct, the kind of smile I use at school when a parent forgets they were supposed to pick up their child an hour ago. "It's so nice to meet you," I say, sliding into the booth beside Henry's mother, who smells like expensive perfume and wears a pearl brooch shaped like a dove.

His father—broad-shouldered, stern jaw, gray at the temples—offers a nod rather than a handshake.

Dinner begins politely enough. I ask about their Thanksgiving plans. His mother talks about the roast and the linens. I sip my water and glance at Henry, who's beaming like this is all going beautifully.

Then his father clears his throat. "Tragic what happened to President Kennedy," he says, voice low and serious.

"But what this country needs now is strength. No more of that softness. No more handouts. A man like Johnson—he'll restore order."

I blink.

Henry's mother dabs the corner of her mouth. "Of course, such a terrible thing. Now, we must carry on."

I nod, trying not to let the silence stretch too long. "Yes, it's been a hard week for everyone. The students were so quiet on Tuesday, it was eerie. They keep asking me why someone would do something like that, and I don't know how to explain it."

Henry gives my knee a squeeze under the table, probably thinking it's reassuring. "You're good with kids," he says with a smile, "always so thoughtful."

His father doesn't smile. "Kids need discipline, not sympathy. That's the problem with all these bleeding hearts—everyone's afraid to stand tall. We need to teach boys to be men."

I want to say something—anything—but I don't. I just take another sip of water and glance out the window at the November dusk.

The whole meal, I try to keep things light—asking about family traditions, commenting on the music playing overhead—but the weight in the room doesn't lift. I smile when it's expected. I laugh when prompted. But it feels like I'm drifting further and further from the booth. From Henry.

Later, when we say our goodbyes, his mother hugs me. "You're very sweet," she says. "Much quieter than I imagined."

I'm not sure if it's a compliment.

I go to bed dizzy with what just happened. The whole evening plays on a loop in my head, out of order—Henry beaming, his father's grim frown, the scent of expensive perfume, the too-smooth way Henry said, "I want you to meet my parents," as if it were a perfectly normal Wednesday night thing to do.

How did I just meet Henry's parents?

I keep telling myself it was just dinner. Just a coincidence. Maybe they were in town for Thanksgiving and he didn't want them to eat alone. That's the only thing that makes sense. Henry and I are still casually—*very* casually—seeing each other. We've gone to a drive-in, a few dinners, our lunches at the bench. That's it. In no way are we at the "meet the parents" stage. We're not even going steady.

So this has to be Henry being polite. That's why he didn't tell me beforehand—because it was all very last-minute. Spontaneous. Harmless.

Right?

Except if it was harmless, why do I feel like I was ambushed?

I replay every smile, every nod, every little performance I gave just to stay afloat in that booth. I think about the way his mother looked me up and down like she was inspecting

The waiter appears with the menus, and I take mine like I'm handling museum glass. Henry, of course, doesn't even need to look.

"We'll take a bottle of Bordeaux," he tells the waiter without even looking at me. I don't like red wine; I'll be polite though. He seems excited about this place.

"You've been here before," I say.

"We come here a lot for work. Meetings and such."

"Fancy," I tease.

He smiles again, but there's something else in his eyes now. Something heavier.

"You know," he says after a pause, "I could get used to this—with you. Dinners like this. A life like this."

My fork froze just shy of my plate.

I smile, maybe a beat too brightly. "Let's not get ahead of ourselves. We haven't even ordered dessert yet."

That gets a proper laugh out of him. I lean back, relieved to have lightened the moment.

Because this is lovely—yes. But serious? I'm not quite there. Not yet.

The rest of the week passes in a blur of spelling tests, bulletin-board turkeys, and too much chalk dust.

By Friday, things feel normal again—until they don't.

The clock above the chalkboard reads 1:42 when Sister Agatha knocks softly on my classroom door. She doesn't open it all the way—just leans her head in, eyes somber and serious.

"Miss Kirchberger, Sister Eileen would like to see you in her office. Right away. It's not just you," she amends quickly, "it's the whole faculty."

My stomach drops. Not out of fear, but something else—something quiet and low and foreboding.

I nod and turn to the class.

Clapping my hands together to shake off the chalk, I say, "Okay, boys and girls. Quiet reading time while I step out for just a minute."

They groan, and a few reach for their books. Teddy is already pretending to read his book upside down.

In the hallway, the world feels muffled. Sister Agatha doesn't say a word. Neither do the other teachers moving quietly toward the front office. Mrs. DeMarco walks beside me. We look at each other, and she just shrugs.

The sound of our heels echoes too loudly against the floor—sharp and unrelenting, like a ticking clock counting down to something terrible.

I can hear a radio, scratchy and distant, growing louder with every step.

And then I hear it.

"*...the president has been shot in Dallas...*"

The voice on the radio is steady, but my hands aren't. I fold them tightly together and squeeze, the sensation helping me ground myself, as Sister Eileen turns it up. No one breathes.

"*...President Kennedy is dead.*"

Gasps. One of the younger teachers cries out like someone just slapped her, then clamps her hand over her mouth. I stand completely still.

My eyes sting; I can't cry though. Not yet. I swallow hard.

He was one of us, beyond politics. Young. Hopeful. Loved by so many.

And now, gone. Just like *that*.

Sister Eileen says we will dismiss early. I walk back to my classroom like I'm trekking through mud.

The kids are still reading—blissfully unaware, still whole. Still in that *before*. *Before* their worlds are about to change.

I watch them for a moment before saying softly, "All right, everyone. Pack up your things. We're going home a little early today."

"Why?" someone asks.

"We'll talk about it on Monday," I say, as gently as I can.

My heart aches. Quietly, I miss Frank—his calm ease, his silly jokes. He'd know exactly what to say right now. Not to fix it—nothing could—but like ointment on a burn, he'd soften the sting. Just enough to breathe again.

When I get home, I turn on the TV—or the idiot box, as Mike so affectionately calls it. What I normally just use to stack books and pile mail flares to life... and with it, the dread of the day. It's all real. There, in technicolor.

Walter Cronkite's voice grave as he says, *"We interrupt this broadcast with a special news bulletin... From Dallas, Texas,: President Kennedy died at 1 p.m. Central Standard Time. Two o'clock Eastern Standard Time.*

He pauses, visibly emotional, removes his glasses, and continues quietly.

"Vice President Lyndon B. Johnson has left the hospital in Dallas but we do not know... to where he has proceeded; presumably he will be taking the oath of office shortly and become the 36th President of the United States. This is all very unprecedented...."
I sink slowly onto the couch.

What does this all mean?

a dress on a rack. The way his father's comments made the air grow colder, heavier, harder to breathe. And the way Henry just sat there, oblivious or indifferent, like he thought I was delighted to be put on display.

Was I supposed to pass some unspoken test?

And what does it say that I tried so hard to pass it?

The part that unsettles me most is how easily I slipped into that version of myself—pleasant, agreeable, good-humored. I was back in the role of "the nice girl." The girl who doesn't rock the boat. The girl who smiles through discomfort and saves her opinions for after dessert.

It makes me wonder: is this the life Henry imagines for me? For *us*? Is there even an *us*?

A quiet table, quiet children, quiet opinions. Pearl brooches and roast beef and nodding politely while someone says something you don't agree with.

I stare at the ceiling for a long time.

There's a version of me who might've wanted all that once. Who thought comfort was the same thing as happiness.

That's not me any more though. The world is changing, and I'm changing with it. Women can do more—*be* more. And I want more for myself than to just smile and nod at the loudest man in the room.

I fall asleep with all those thoughts still circling in my head like autumn leaves caught in a restless wind, the city a quiet hum outside my window.

By the time I wake again, the leaves have turned brittle and brown and the air crisp enough to bite. Thanksgiving has arrived, and yesterday is already slipping into a distant—if decidedly uncomfortable—memory. Or at least that's what I'm telling myself. Today, I'm choosing to lean into the homey traditions of the holiday and the familiar comfort they bring.

Mom drops a spoon—"Oh! Company," she says with a laugh, delivering her overdone joke like it's brand new. I roll my eyes inwardly, but the corners of my mouth still pull into a smile.

Dad's already at the table, carving slices off the turkey with the same methodical precision he applies to everything. Michael Jr. hovers nearby, angling for the first piece. Karen shows off her paper pilgrim hat to anyone who will look, already starting on her next masterpiece before we've even sat down. Theresa is "helping" Annette mash the potatoes—which really means eating them straight off the spoon and occasionally sneaking Denise a lick in her playpen.

Annette catches my eye over Theresa's head and mouths *help me*, though she's laughing, clearly loving every second of it.

Once we're all seated, Dad proudly shows off a new coin he found in one of his vending machines, passing it around for each of the kids to admire.

Mike launches into a story about a guy causing trouble at the factory—"I'm gonna have to straighten him out," he says, half amused, half serious. But mostly serious.

Annette laughs and asks, for the third year in a row, why we always have sauerkraut on the table and who's actually eating it.

"Just leave it, Annette," Mike replies.

She flutters her eyelashes at him, which I'm pretty sure is her version of an eye roll.

As we're cleaning the dinner plates, a few kernels of corn slip onto the table, sparking a memory in Karen.

"Hey, Mom, remember that time you went cuckoo over the corn?" she says, barely getting it out between giggles.

Annette gives her a faux-stern look. "I didn't go cuckoo— I just wasn't going to stand for dry, sad-looking corn!"

That gets everyone laughing, and Annette dives into a story about how she always makes sure the corn she gets is perfect—how sometimes the ears look a little worse for the wear, and how she won't stand for it. Once, she even followed the man at the farm stand into the field to pick them herself. The kids act out the scene in exaggerated detail, and by the time they're done, we're all laughing to the point of tears.

"It wasn't the first time, and it won't be the last. And I can't help but notice every last kernel was eaten then," she adds with a grin.

After dinner, we gather around the table to play one of our favorite card games, Sevens. The kids, not fully grasping the rules, pool their pennies and form a team to try and beat the adults. There's more giggling than strategy, and somehow that just makes it better.

By the time dessert is served, Mom is back in the kitchen, softly singing "Wooden Heart." The sound drifts into the room—familiar, warm, and steady. It's one of her favorites and it feels like whipped cream on apple pie—sweet and comforting. The perfect topping to a lovely day.

My pumpkin pie sits mostly untouched next to mom's homemade apple strudel and Annette's lemon cake. I'm not offended—it's hard to compete with something that smells like a hug and tastes like love and memories.

I sink into it all.

The laughter, the closeness, the steady hum of voices—it wraps around me like a well-worn sweater, broken in just right. It's exactly what I needed. The comfort is so complete I nearly choke up.

I picture Jackie—her first holiday without her husband, so soon after losing him. The image catches in my chest.

And suddenly, I feel overwhelmed with gratitude.

For this family of mine. For this noise. This table. This life.

And then, unbidden, I wonder how Frank would fit into all of this. The thought pulls me upright.

I softly laugh at myself—because I already know the answer. He'd fit in just fine.

Thanksgiving break was desperately needed. While enjoying the leftovers at home, I realized I'd left my scarf at Mike and Annette's. I called Mike—he said he'd already passed it along to Mom and Dad. So I rang Mom, and we ended up chatting for a bit about Thanksgiving—how good the food was and how nice it was to have everyone together. She told me she had the scarf, and I said I'd hop on the subway after school tomorrow to swing by and pick it up.

On the walk from the subway, I pass the deli. *Our* deli. And there he is—Henry—stepping out with a steaming coffee in hand.

"Well, hello stranger," I say, narrowly dodging the cup.

He grins. "What a pleasant surprise! You've made it back to our deli—back to our humble beginnings."

I laugh. "I've missed it. A little nostalgia goes a long way."

"What brings you over here?" he asks.

"Just making a quick stop at my parents' place."

He pauses for a moment "I should walk you," he offers.

"Sure, I wouldn't mind the company." The discomfort I was feeling from our last date is starting to melt away.

The brownstone apartment looks just the same. My parents are out front on the stoop in sweaters, hands wrapped around steaming mugs of apple cider. They spot us approaching—me with Henry by my side—and there's a pause. Not quite surprised, but definitely not expecting him.

My mom offers a polite smile. My dad gives a small nod, his eyes darting between the two of us, trying to read the situation.

Henry, naturally, is all charm.

"Mr. and Mrs. Kirchberger," he says, stepping forward and offering his hand to my dad. "It's so nice to finally meet you. Hope you've been keeping warm. I'm Henry Ashford, I'm sure Trudy's mentioned me."

They hesitate for a beat, then my dad reaches out to shake his hand. My mom's smile softens.

At first, there's a flicker of wariness—polite yet still reserved. But Henry has a way of smoothing things over. He compliments the cider, asks about their Thanksgiving, makes an easy joke about the chill in the air. Slowly, they begin to thaw.

Just like the air between us did. Was this his plan? Did he just trick me into introducing him to my parents too?

It seems Henry is a little more scheming than I realized.

Then I see a flicker of recognition light up Dad's face. "I finally placed the name. *Ashford*—like Ashford's Law Firm." My father snaps his fingers, pleased with himself. "That's a funny coincidence."

"No coincidence, sir. We're one and the same." Henry's smile tilts just enough to suggest confidence, with a conspiratorial edge, as though he's letting Dad in on a secret. "That's my father's firm. Eventually it'll be *Ashford & Sons*—or *Ashford & Ashford*. We haven't settled on the name yet."

My father chuckles. "That's a well-known firm. Branches all over, if I'm not mistaken."

"That's right," Henry replies smoothly. "He's always expanding. I'm fortunate to be learning from such a successful man." His voice softens on that last line, affectionate in a way that's almost sweet—like his admiration for his father is genuine, not just rehearsed.

"I thought you worked at a bank," I chime in, laughing

Henry lets out a booming laugh that seems to fill the block.

"Ah, yes, the bank," Henry says with mock seriousness, as though indulging a child's guess. "Close enough. That's why I always say: leave the dull details to me. You'll enjoy the benefits without having to worry about the tedium."

I laugh with him. "Careful, Henry. If you keep all the tedium for yourself, I might start to think you enjoy it."

The look on my father's face as it all plays out before him says more than words ever could. This—Henry, the name, the promise of inheritance—is everything he could ever want in a match for me.

There's something about the way everything unfolded that leaves me feeling… off balance.

By the time I get home, I know exactly what I need: Patty, Caroline, and a night of laughter.

I call them both and tell them I'm in dire need of some girls' time—which is true—and we make plans for Friday night.

It's only after I hang up that I realize: they still haven't seen the apartment

About time, really.

Afterward, I glance at the stack of papers on my desk, then at the empty space where Frank's last letter had been.

Trudy,

I sat with your letter for a while before writing back—not because I didn't want to, but because I wanted to say the right thing. You deserve that, especially after a day like that.

I was at the deli when I heard. The small one on the corner, the one that always smells faintly like pickles and burnt toast. The man behind the counter turned up the radio and just stood there, frozen, holding a loaf of rye. We all listened, not moving. I think some moments freeze the world in place—and this was one of them.

I thought of you right away. Your students. Your heart. I wanted to be sitting beside you, even if we just listened to the silence together. Some things don't need to be talked over. Just sat with.

I'm glad you're going to Long Island. The noise, the pie, the kids climbing on furniture and each other—it sounds like the kind of chaos that might ease the ache a little. I've always found that the sound of children laughing is one of the only things louder than grief.

As for Thanksgiving—I usually do a little volunteer work if I can, then eat with whoever's around. Last year I had dinner with two neighbors, a beagle named Norman, and a lasagna that could've doubled as a doorstop. Not sure what this year will look like yet, but I'm open to suggestions.

Oh—and the cat? How did you know about him? I swear to you, this thing wore a crooked ear like a fedora and gave me the kind of look that said, "You owe me two cans of tuna and I know where your mother lives." I still cross the street when I see him. No shame in self-preservation.

Write again, if you feel like it.

I'd like that.

Take gentle care of yourself.

Yours,

Frank

I haven't written to him in a few days.

Life's been busy, sure, but that's not the reason. I was cracked wide open when JFK was killed, my emotions spilled out everywhere; I am still trying to make sense of it all. One thing I did feel clearly was how much I yearned to be near him—how much I knew he would ease the sadness that wrapped around me like an invisible blanket. It simultaneously settles me and unsettles me that I feel so drawn to him, and so connected to him. Looking at his letter again, I feel it all. His words comfort me more than I know what to do with.

I ache to talk to him, and my pen moves like it has a life of its own.

Frank,

You have no idea how much your letter meant to me. Or maybe you do—that wouldn't surprise me. You seem to know just how to thread the needle between letting me feel what I'm feeling and still managing to make me laugh with a lasagna-doorstop or a mobster cat.

(And I need you to know I read "You owe me two cans of tuna and I know where your mother lives" out loud and laughed so hard I startled the guy in the apartment next to mine. He knocked once on

the wall, disapprovingly. I knocked back, apologetically. We've reached stalemate.)

Long Island was loud and sticky and perfect. There was whipped cream in places it shouldn't be, and Karen somehow managed to draw a turkey that looked more like a depressed pelican, but the kids were happy, and for a little while, that made me happy too.

The ache is still there, of course. I think it might be a permanent resident at this point——pays no rent, contributes nothing, but insists on staying. But your letter helped. Really helped. Like a lamp switched on in a dim room.

I hope you didn't spend Thanksgiving with just Norman again (though I wouldn't blame you——he sounds like excellent company). I wish we could've shared it.

Anyway, thanks for writing. For making me laugh when I needed it. For being exactly who you are.

Don't forget to write again soon, if you feel like it.

Yours,

Trudy

P.S. Do not feed that cat. I don't want to find out he's unionized.

By the time Friday rolls around, the apartment smells like cinnamon and cloves—spiked apple cider bubbling gently on the stove. I've set out three mismatched mugs and even lit a candle, the one I've been "saving" for no real reason.

Patty and Caroline arrive in a swirl of cold air, laughter, and too many layers, their cheeks red from the cold. Patty's holding a box of cookies and kicking off her shoes like she's lived here for years. They come bursting through the door like a gust of life, and I can feel how much I've missed them.

I give them a modest tour of my little space, and they "ooh" and "ah" in all the right places—over my tiny bookshelf, the wobbly kitchen table, the framed postcard I found at Coney Island.

"So," Caroline says, raising an eyebrow over her cider. "Tell me about Mr. Henry."

She adds a little shimmy for good measure, the kind that makes Patty snort and me groan into my mug.

I launch into a full-scale rant—how I ran into him outside the deli, how he oh-so-casually offered to walk me home, how my parents just *happened* to be sitting outside with apple cider like we were walking straight into the front of a scenic greeting card—only with more scheming and less glitter.

They're leaning so far forward I half-expect one of them to tip off the couch. I'm afraid to even *mention* the ambush of his parents the Wednesday before Thanksgiving, for fear they'll both combust. By the time I finish, they're just blinking at me.

"So let me get this straight," Patty says slowly, "you ran into Henry by accident, and now your parents are in love with him?"

"It wasn't a setup," I insist. "He just... walked me home."

"Mmhmm," Caroline says, deadpan. "And I just accidentally wore lipstick to the grocery store today. Try again."

"Well—" I drag the word out longer than necessary. "I *did* run into him by accident, definitely. But the walk to my parents'... yeah. That felt orchestrated."

Then... then I tell them about Frank.

They know him, but don't really *know* him.

I tell them about the letters. About how we've been writing. How easy it is with him. How I don't have to try so hard to be clever, or charming, or anything at all.

As I speak, I see something shift in their faces. The teasing falls away, replaced by something quieter—soft curiosity, maybe. A flicker of recognition. Their faces soften, but mine warms—suddenly aware of how much I've let him in.

I clear my throat. "Okay—your turn, ladies."

Patty talks about school. She tries to play it off like it's nothing, but I can tell—it's a reflex now, the way she's learned to shrink herself after too many people at work claimed her ideas as their own. Still, she lights up when she talks about her classes, and I know she's going to be a phenomenal nurse, no matter how used to downplaying herself she's become.

Caroline rolls her eyes and launches into a rant about her boss. "He keeps calling me 'honey.' I keep telling him, I don't type ninety words a minute just for him to keep calling me *honey*, honey!"

We all dissolve into laughter, cider sloshing dangerously close to the edge of our mugs.

It's a night I think we all needed.

The next day, I call Henry. I tell him—politely—that with the weather being what it is, it might be best if we paused our weekly lunch dates for a while. It's December for heaven's sake, and unless he's bringing me a thick fur coat every time I see him, I'm worried I'll turn into a popsicle halfway through our sandwiches.

Not that I'd ever say that to him, of course—knowing Henry, he'd show up next time with three different coat options for me to choose from.

I snort to myself.

Who am I kidding? There wouldn't be three options. He'd have one—and he'd tell me to wear it, even if it was hideous.

But it would keep me warm.

There's a beat of silence. Then he suggests we try something different instead—maybe early dinners, somewhere cozy and warm.

"It can still be on Wednesdays," he says quickly. "Or maybe we move it to the weekends?"

He says it like it's a compromise. Like he's adjusting.

I'm starting to think he doesn't think he likes change very much.

Or maybe… he just doesn't like change that doesn't come from *him*.

I don't want to give up my weekends. Not every weekend. I know how this goes—once we start, he'll want it to continue.

Just like the lunches.

I sigh quietly, into the receiver. He couldn't have expected us to do this all year long. We'd cancel lunch if it rained— this is the same thing.

Just weather.

Just shifting plans.

Just… a little space.

"All right," I say. "Dinner Wednesday sounds fine."

And it does.

It sounds *fine*.

I decide to take the rest of the day to finish *The Feminine Mystique* and grade papers, except my mind keeps wandering.

Nothing like a little Betty Friedan and a pile of half-finished essays to make you question everything—especially your taste in men.

I should be focusing on sentence structure. Instead, I keep hearing Frank's voice in my head.

This is ridiculous, I think to myself. *Just call him.*

I stare at the phone for longer than I'd like to admit. It's silly, really. Just a call.

I reach for the receiver, then pull my hand back. Then reach again.

The rotary clicks beneath my fingers, each number dragging like it's trying to give me time to change my mind. The soft whir as it spins back feels louder than it should.

By the time I finish the last digit, my heart is tapping out a rhythm that has nothing to do with nerves and everything to do with him.

I bring the receiver to my ear.

One ring.

Two.

"Hello?"

It's his voice.

Warm. Familiar.

What was I nervous about?

It's just Frank.

"And how are you faring with the cold, Mr. Madden? Because I, for one, can't stand it."

I hear a smile in his voice before he even says a word—he knows it's me. And just like that, we're off.

Three and a half hours later, the sun is dipping low in the sky, and somehow, we're watching it together—miles apart, but in sync.

"All right," I sigh, not wanting to. "I should probably go have dinner."

"Why don't you go with me?" he says. "I'm hungry too."

I smile.

"That sounds great. Want to grab a slice somewhere?"

"You read my mind," he says.

We pick a spot not too far from me—his voice warm as he gives the cross streets like it's a secret only we share. I hang up, change into something warmer, and throw on my coat.

The evening's cold, and crisp in a way that feels good. I walk with purpose, my heart a little lighter than it's been in days.

And there, just ahead, is the warm glow of the pizzeria windows.

The bell over the door jingles as I step inside. The place smells like oregano and comfort. Frank's already there, leaning casually against the counter with his hands in his pockets.

"You made it," he says, straightening up when he sees me.

"Wouldn't miss it. I was promised pizza and good company." I glance around. "Let's hope at least one of those shows up."

I wink at him.

He smirks. "Wow. Five minutes in and already insulting your dinner date." He clutches his chest like he's been wounded.

We order—two slices and a Coke each—and slide into a booth near the window. The kind with the red-and-white checkered table and the slightly sticky surface. The glass bottle is cold against hands but feels nice—in a room that's surprisingly warm.

"So," I say, unwrapping a napkin and placing one on my knee—I'm still a lady, after all, "where did we leave off?"

"I believe I was telling you what it's like to try and write on a deadline," he says, leaning back slightly, a lazy smile playing on his lips.

Breathtaking.

"Oh, right. The tragic plight of the tortured writer," I say, mock-sympathetic. "How *ever* do you survive?"

He grins. "Mostly on black coffee and mild panic."

I take a bite of pizza—still warm enough to sting. "Sounds familiar. Except I have thirty third-graders and a red pen."

"Same thing, really. Just different handwriting," he says, pulling at his already loose collar like it's bothering him.

I laugh.

And it feels effortless, like we've done this a hundred times before—even though we haven't.

When he walks me home, I feel a closeness that's like taking a deep breath.

It fills me completely—settling somewhere deep, comforting the cracks in me I didn't even know were aching.

We linger outside my apartment, and I fidget with my keys, trying to make the moment last just a little longer.

The street is quiet in that dreamy, late-evening kind of way—stoops dimly lit, a dog barking faintly in the distance, the scent of someone's dinner still hanging in the air. A breeze picks up, rustling the leaves that have gathered near the curb, and somewhere down the block, a radio hums softly through an open window, a familiar tune that makes me want to hum along.

When I finally look up from my hands, he's already looking at me—his eyes steady, holding mine.

It's one of those moments that feels suspended in time, like everything around us slows to a hush.

I don't know who leans in first.

Then—suddenly—our lips meet.

It's not long.

But it's enough. A part of me wonders if it would ever be enough.

Like a lifeline, extended beyond my own body—gentle, anchoring, and entirely unexpected.

My cheeks are flushed, and it feels like my mind is racing just as fast as my heart.

"Goodnight, Trudy," he whispers into my ear. Then he kisses my cheek again.

It sends shivers down my spine, and I lean into him without thinking.

"Goodnight, Frank," I say, smiling. "Don't forget to write."

I'm pretty sure a cloud carries me inside.

I sit down on the couch with my coat and purse still on, barely aware if I've even closed the door behind me. *I did.*

I touch my fingers to my lips.

I could swear they're still tingling—a vivid, electric trace of his kiss, like the sensation is imprinted there. Real. Unmistakable.

Something stirs in me—a quiet hunger I didn't expect.

And suddenly, I can't wait to see him again.

Chapter 7

"At Christmas, all roads lead home." — *Marjorie Holmes*

It feels like all of December, the kids are already half out the door.

There's an energy in the air that crackles with excitement and anticipation.

Trying to keep them focused on the task at hand feels like an award-winning effort every *single* day.

I find myself counting down to Christmas break right along with them—not because I don't love being with them, just because I'm exhausted.

Completely, head-to-toe, soul-deep exhausted.

The last day before Christmas break feels more like babysitting at a carnival than a school day. The kids come in practically vibrating with sugar and anticipation—coats half-off, hair full of static, a few trailing glitter like they've wandered in from Santa's workshop. *It's 8 a.m., how are they already covered in glitter?*

We make it through the morning—just barely. I do my best to keep things semi-structured: math with candy cane counters, reading time with Christmas poems. By the afternoon however, it's clear no one is absorbing anything except frosting.

At 2:05, the party officially begins—blessedly sanctioned, 25 whole minutes of chaos wrapped in red and green napkins.

Each child brings something: foil-wrapped cookies, bowls of pretzels, fudge someone's grandmother probably made with condensed milk and a prayer. They're all so proud of their treats, holding them up like prized possessions, eager for me—and everyone else—to take a bite.

Cups of red punch appear on every surface. Someone even brought a box of those little marshmallow Santas that look and taste like rubber, yet somehow they disappear in minutes.

There's a record player in the corner, and we take turns putting on carols from a stack of dusty sleeves. "Jingle Bell Rock" plays twice in a row, followed by a slightly warped "O Come All Ye Faithful." No one seems to mind.

I float between tables, wiping spills, tying ribbons, pretending not to see when Jimmy sneaks an extra cookie into his pocket. It's loud, it's sticky, and it smells like sugar and crayons—but it's joy. Real, unfiltered, giggling joy.

When the clock reads 2:30, I clap my hands, and to my surprise, they quiet quickly.

"All right," I say, reaching for the worn red book on my desk. "Gather 'round. I brought a little something from home."

It's *The Night Before Christmas.*

They settle at my feet, cross-legged and wide-eyed. Some still chewing. Some still bouncing a little from the party buzz. But there's a hush—just enough for me to begin.

"'Twas the night before Christmas, when all through the house…"

I'm surprised by how intently they listen—especially considering most of them are now primarily made of sugar.

They still fidget in their spots, of course. Someone knocks over a cup, a cookie crumbles to the floor.

But for a moment, it still lingers—that quiet magic.

The kind you only really feel when you're eight and it's almost Christmas.

We have five minutes until the bell. I let them chatter, pack up their crayon-scribbled cards, and bounce in their seats. I just sit there, letting it all wash over me. I'm starting to understand why this has become Mike's favorite holiday.

Because eventually the room will be quiet again.

But this—this part—I'll remember.

When I get home, I'm wiped. I still need to wrap all my gifts, but something catches my eye: a letter from Frank hidden under a pile of mail.

Dear Trudy,

I haven't been able to stop thinking about the other night.

You, laughing at my tragic deadline tales and trying not to burn your mouth on pizza (and failing, might I add).

You, telling me to "be charming, not clever"—and then letting me walk you home anyway.

I'd call the night ordinary, except that it wasn't. Not at all.

I hope I didn't catch you off guard. I meant it to be gentle, that kiss—in case you were wondering.

Also: I think I owe you a slice. You were too busy laughing to finish your second one (I noticed), and I'm not above using that as an excuse to see you again.

Don't forget to write me back if you'd like. Or don't—though I hope you will.

Tell me how your kids reacted to the cookie Santas you were planning on bringing for them.

Tell me what your parents are like when you're not watching.

Tell me anything at all. I'm listening.

—Frank

P.S. You've got the kind of laugh that could stop a man mid-sentence.

(Ask me how I know.)

That man. What he does to my heart. I swear he makes it forget how to beat properly.

I'm exhausted from the school Christmas party—bone-deep tired. But I promised Henry dinner, and it *is* Wednesday after all. My mind keeps drifting to lists: gifts to wrap, papers to grade before the break ends, groceries to buy. Still, a promise is a promise.

I slip into a green dress—festive enough—and briefly consider topping it with a reindeer antler headband that I wore for the school party. At first, I set it aside, but the thought lingers. With the holiday rush, I can't even remember the name of the restaurant Henry chose. Luckily, I don't have to; he insists on picking me up so I won't have to walk in the cold. A thoughtful gesture, and one less thing for me to remember.

Sure enough, his cherry-red car gleams down the street, impossible to miss. He's right on time. After a final glance in the mirror, I swipe the headband onto my hair anyway. It's the holidays—why not be a little silly?

I wave as he pulls up, then slide into the passenger seat.

"What on earth are you wearing?" His brows climb so high I think they might vanish into his hairline.

"It's a dress, Henry. I figured a sophisticated man like yourself would recognize one. Or do your personal shoppers handle that for you?" I tease.

"I mean that—on your head."

"You mean my hair? Thank you, I styled it just for you." I primp it dramatically, but he isn't amused. Which, of course, makes me want to tease him more.

"Trudy," he says firmly, "you can't wear that to dinner."

"Why ever not? It's festive."

"It's ridiculous, that's what it is. Did you wear that to school? For the kids, maybe? Did you forget you had it on?" He sounds as if he's trying to offer me an excuse, a way out.

"Well, yes. But I thought it would be cute."

"You're a grown woman. What if there are partners at the restaurant? Is that the impression you want to give?"

"I guess not…"

"Good. You can just leave it in the car. Now we can have a lovely evening. I've missed you. I even brought a small gift."

I bite back a smile. Imagine that—festivity as a scandal.

"I have something small for you as well," I say, my voice smaller than I intend, though I try to add a little joy to it. "It's not much."

"I don't expect it to be." His smile is tight, practiced.

The rest of the night goes fine enough. The restaurant is grand, dressed with enormous ornaments dangling from the ceiling. I've always loved how restaurants and department stores deck themselves out at Christmas—so immersive, as if the building itself caught the season's joy and couldn't resist showing it off. Yet the sparkle only reminds me of my antler headband, lying abandoned on Henry's passenger seat. Silly, yes. But frustrating, too.

Henry gives me a pearl brooch in the shape of an angel. An... interesting choice. I smile and thank him. My gift— a vintage pen I found on sale—he seems to genuinely like, which is at least a relief.

By the time I arrive home, the weight of the evening sits heavy on my chest. I like childish things sometimes. I don't want to feel ashamed for that. I know Henry means well, but it often leaves me feeling small.

With a sigh, I drop the brooch on my dresser, set *Rockin' Around the Christmas Tree* spinning on the record player, and pour myself a spiked hot chocolate. Then I slip the headband back on and twirl around my apartment, festive as I damn well please.

It's my first Christmas in my very own apartment, but in our family, it's all about Christmas Eve.

And even though this is the first year I'm not living at home, there's no way I'm missing the magic with the kids. I'll make my own traditions someday—but these? These I'll hold on to for as long as I can.

My parents pick me up in the van early on Christmas Eve, and we head to Long Island with my modest collection of gifts for the kids—plus one birthday present for Karen. Having a late December birthday must be impossibly hard, and I never want her to think I forgot.

Combined with their gifts—and the ones from Santa—we pile everything into the back and make our way to buy the Christmas tree. I'm not even sure when this tradition started—I love it though.

Mike and Annette take the kids out to look for Santa in the sky while we sneak out to get the tree. We deliver and decorate it, arrange the gifts, and make sure everything is in place so that, when the kids walk back in, it feels like Christmas has happened.

It's absolutely magic.

Just like every year, the ornaments are laid out on the coffee table, waiting for us. We get to work quickly— because that's part of the tradition too.

And so, in a flurry of tinsel, laughter, and eggnog secretly poured into coffee cups, we build Christmas from scratch.

When the front door opens again, we freeze—just for a second, all of us mid-motion, holding our breath.

Then we hear it:

A gasp.

A delighted squeal.

The sound of tiny feet thundering across the floor.

"Santa came!" Karen clasps her hands to her chest, spinning in place like she's trying to take it all in at once.

"Woah!" Michael Jr. gasps, eyes wide as saucers.

Theresa's already crouched by the tree, examining the ornaments like they're museum pieces.

And little Denise lets out a shriek of pure glee, wobbling on her little legs and patting the wrapped boxes like they're alive.

Their awe is so big, it fills the room—bouncing off the tinsel, shimmering in the lights, lingering in the corners like warm air after a snowfall.

I watch them, heart full. This—this—is the kind of magic you don't grow out of.

They're happy as can be—playing with their new toys, singing carols with Mom, and covered in wrapping paper like it's their own personal snowstorm.

"So, do you have anything fun planned for your break?" Annette asks as she bends to scoop up a pile of ribbon.

"I've got a few parties I'm supposed to make an appearance at," I say, joining her in the clean-up effort. "It'll be nice to see friends. Something about this time of year—I love how it brings people together."

She gives me a look. "I suppose so…" she trails off, then lifts an eyebrow. "Anyone special you'll be seeing?"

I smile, maybe too quickly. "I'm not sure, honestly. But we'll see where the week takes us."

I stay over on Christmas Eve and go to church with them in the morning. Afterward, I head back home and settle into the quiet of my apartment.

My stocking is still hanging—crookedly—over the television set. The small tree in the corner glows softly, and the Christmas lights strung across the room give off just enough cheer.

I sit for a while, basking in the memory of the joy I just helped create.

I pour myself a cup of hot apple cider, munch on some Linzer tarts, turn on some Christmas music, and let it all wrap around me like a blanket.

I may not have traditions of my own just yet, but this—this feels like a good start.

I'm already tired—but excited, too. The idea of going out into the cold sounds *awful*, but when Patty invited me to this little New Year's Eve shindig, I'd been in a much more social mood. Clearly, I'd forgotten just how bitter the New York cold can be. She'd also mentioned that everyone would be there. And the way she said everyone? I could only assume she meant Frank.

So, *obviously*, I'm going.

None of my clothes feel right. I wanted to stand out in a room full of people— we're going to a pub, not the Ritz—still, how else would Frank even notice me? I know I'm overthinking. I know. But I think I'm just excited.

Excited to see him.

We haven't seen each other since we kissed. And the idea of seeing him again makes my stomach flip with anticipation.

By the time I get there, the front windows are fogged with warmth and breath, glowing golden from the inside out. There's a hand-painted sign above the door that reads *Sláinte*, that's now slightly crooked—like it's had one too many itself. The door sticks just enough to require a tug before it swings open to reveal a world of noise and heat.

Inside, the wood-paneled walls are stained dark from decades of smoke and stories. The bar is lined with regulars—men in hats and wool coats, women in festive pins and lipstick worn just for tonight. A few wear paper party hats that have already begun to droop, and I hope that's not an omen of what the year has to bring.

The jukebox hums gently in the corner, playing something familiar I can't quite name. I pause, trying to place it—and then I spot them. My group. My people.

I shuffle my way through the crowd, dodging elbows and laughter, and pull them both into quick hugs.

"It's freezing out there," I say, brushing snow from my coat.

"Ugh, I know," Patty groans. "But this place is great, and close by. So it's totally worth the frostbite."

I narrow my eyes. "We'll see about that—if they can make me a hot toddy, I might forgive you for making me go out in the cold."

We laugh, and I shrug off my coat, joining the sea of friends scattered around the room. Coats pile beside stools and booths, hands wrap around mugs of Irish coffee or pints of dark ale, and everyone's cheeks are red from the cold or the whiskey—or both.

I scan the room casually, trying not to be obvious. Looking for someone.

But he's not here.

I try to squash the disappointment curling in my chest, like cold air seeping in through a cracked window. I shake it off and focus on the warmth in the room, the music, the chatter and the company. Still—I can't help glancing toward the door.

Just once more.

The hot toddy does wonders to warm my bones and heighten my spirits. The night unfolds in bursts of laughter and the clink of glasses. Someone starts a countdown—an hour too early—and someone else spills their drink trying to dance between tables. Patty introduces me to a friend of a friend who works in radio and insists we'd get along. Caroline tells a story so wildly inappropriate we nearly choke on our drinks.

By the time the real counting down begins we're all in fantastic spirits. We count down. Ten, nine, eight…

And then it's midnight.

Someone kisses my cheek. Patty hugs me tight. Caroline tosses confetti into the air. I have no idea where she got it from.

I gather my things and get ready to leave, a laugh still playing on my lips as I push open the sticky tavern door. I'm so focused on wrestling it open that I nearly walk straight into someone.

"Oh—sorry!" I say absently, brushing hair from my face.

"I'd scold you for not paying attention," a familiar voice replies, "but I'm the one who's terribly late."

Frank.

The laugh dies on my lips. I blink up at him, stunned—and then completely, ridiculously overjoyed.

"Late?" I say, recovering with a smirk. "Honey, you missed the countdown altogether."

"Maybe," he says, breath fogging slightly in the cold. "But I was hoping I could still wish you a happy new year."

He says it sheepishly, like he's not sure he deserves the moment.

He nods towards the door. "Do you have to leave?"

"It's late…" I say, but I don't move. I linger.

"Why don't I walk you home?"

"Yes, why don't you?" I smile. But then I pause. "Wait— you haven't even gone in yet. Don't you want to say hello?"

"To who? Just so I can just as quickly say goodbye?"

"Oh, I'm sure they'd still like to see you. Even if just for a minute."

He shakes his head softly. "I'd rather spend my time with you. Walk you home, if you don't mind."

"Of course I don't." I glance at him, cheeks warm despite the chill. "It may just end up being the highlight of my evening."

And just like that, a night that was already wonderful… somehow reaches new heights. Nineteen-sixty-four is already looking like it's full of promise.

We walk together—not quite holding hands, but close enough that our arms keep brushing. And each time, I notice.

"So," I say, casting him a sidelong glance, "what made you so late? Did you have another date?"

I raise an eyebrow, teasing.

He throws his head back and laughs. "No—well, unless you count *The Daily News* as a date. I found an error that had to be fixed before tomorrow—well, today now." He smiles at me. "By the time I got back, I sat down for a second and… next thing I know, I'm waking up at 11:30. I high-tailed it down here to try and catch yo—well, to get to the party," he says, nodding toward the pub we're now walking away from.

"You wanted to see me," I sing-song, nudging him.

"Oh, absolutely," he says without missing a beat. "That's the only reason I moved like a bullet—to try and catch you before you left."

"Well, you got me."

I say it lightly, but the moment it leaves my lips, I feel how true it really is.

"Good," he says. "I wouldn't want to start the year off wrong."

I glance up at him. "And how exactly would it be started off wrong?"

"Without you," he says—quickly, like it should've been obvious all along.

Maybe it's the liquor that's made me bold—or just the way he's looking at me—but I stop walking and turn to face him, a grin already forming.

"Since you missed the countdown..." I say, tilting my head.

His brow lifts, curious.

I put up a gloved hand.

"Five..."

He smiles, catching on.

"Four..." I step a little closer.

"Three..." His eyes don't leave mine.

"Two..." The whole world seems to hush.

"One."

And then I kiss him—soft and sure and full of all the promise the new year deserves.

Things really pick up with Frank after that. We don't have it in us to deny our feelings anymore. It felt like a gravitational pull—one of us always drawn to the other.

We speak on the phone every night after work. We still write letters, of course, either way our nightly chats became a lifeline on the long days.

We talk about the world—how we want to see every inch of it, and the quiet ways we've each tried to change it. We make silly travel plans like schoolchildren with crushes. We talked about how we feel. We joke about what our children might look like.

Sometimes we fall asleep on the phone together. Other times we cook dinner while we talk.

And every night, without fail, we end the call the same way:

"Goodnight. And don't forget to write."

Somewhere between the phone calls and letters with Frank, I keep finding ways to dodge Henry's dinner invitations. I know I need to end it, but part of me hopes that if I keep sidestepping him long enough, he'll finally take the hint. He doesn't. If anything, each phone call makes his irritation more obvious, the sharpness bleeding through the receiver with every clipped word.

But it doesn't feel like a priority, not when my days are so easily filled with Frank. Thinking about him. Talking to him. Writing letters. Rereading the ones he's sent. Frank has a way of slipping into everything, turning the ordinary into something bright. And compared to that, Henry feels like an obligation I can no longer bring myself to make time for.

Frank and I have grown close enough that I decide to invite him to Denise's first birthday.

He got along so well with the kids the last time he saw them—and after all the stories I've told, I think I've made them larger than life in his eyes.

He agrees without hesitation, saying he's looking forward to it.

We arrive together at Mike and Annette's house. My parents are already there, and the party is in full swing— balloons taped to doorways, toys scattered underfoot, laughter spilling out of the house and into the cold January street.

The house is packed with family and friends tucked in every corner. There's something about the familiar chaos—the coats on the banister, the clatter in the kitchen, the soundtrack of kids yelling and music playing too low to hear clearly—that wraps around me like a cozy scarf on a cold day. To some it might feel suffocating, but to me it's a warmth that comforts.

"Frank, it's good to see you again," Mike says, shaking his hand firmly.

"Thanks for having me," Frank replies. "Trudy's told me so much about everyone—I figured it was time I saw it for myself. I know I met everyone briefly over the summer, but I don't feel like I really got to know the kids the way she describes them."

"Don't trust anything she says," Mike grins. "Unless it's flattering. Then *always* believe it."

I spot Annette in the kitchen, Denise on her hip and a tray of cupcakes teetering dangerously in her other hand. I rush over just in time to catch them before they slide to the floor.

"Okay, put me to work! What needs to get done?" I say, grabbing the tray holding cupcakes, which I now notice have cute little snowflakes on them.

"Be careful what you wish for," Annette warns, already handing me a list and pointing with her elbow.

I pull Frank into the mix, and together we start using streamers to decorate Denise's high chair.

Well, that's the plan—except Frank seems more interested in twisting them into a makeshift necklace for me instead.

We're both laughing, doing our best to make it look semi-presentable while trying not to draw too much attention to ourselves.

It's lopsided and a little chaotic—but it's cheerful. And I realize how happy I am to have Frank here, in a room with people I love so completely.

She has us make a sign next: "Our Little Snowflake is Turning One."

We lay out a large sheet of paper on the dining table and get to work with paints and brushes.

As it turns out, Frank's a bit of an artist. What was supposed to be a modest birthday sign quickly becomes a full winter wonderland—snowmen with carrot noses, delicate snowflakes, icicles hanging off the corners. He paints the lettering in a swirling script layered with blue and white, soft edges fading like frost on a window.

I sit beside him, holding my paintbrush, feeling more than a little useless. I'm transfixed—by the painting, yes, but mostly by him.

There's something about the way his brow furrows in concentration, the way his arm moves smoothly across the page. He looks good focused. *Too good.*

He finishes a snowflake and looks up, catching me staring.

"What?" he asks, a soft smile tugging at the corner of his mouth.

"Nothing," I say, feigning casual. "You just look... focused."

"Well, I'd like it to look nice for your niece," he says, dipping his brush into white. "And... I wouldn't mind if your family liked me either."

Before I can reply, he leans over and taps the end of my nose with his brush, leaving a little white dot behind.

I laugh and swipe a bit of blue paint across his cheek. He feigns shock, and I stick out my tongue at him.

The sign is still drying when the kids come bursting in.

"Whoa!" Michael Jr. says, eyes wide. "Did you make all that?"

"Frank did most of it," I say.

Michael Jr. looks at him with sudden reverence. "Not too bad."

"She helped more than she's letting on," Frank says with a wink.

Theresa inspects the lettering like a tiny art critic. "It's very fancy," she declares, then slips her hand into his like it's the most natural thing in the world.

Karen pulls a party hat out of nowhere and insists he wear it. Frank doesn't hesitate—he bends down so she can place it squarely on his head, then gives her a dramatic bow.

Mike walks past, carrying a bowl of chips. He glances at me, then at Frank, and gives a short nod. "He's a good sport," he says under his breath, almost like a compliment disguised as a warning. "Annette likes him."

I smile. "Yeah. Me too."

And just like that, Frank is folded into the day—as if he's always been here, laughing in the living room, holding Denise while she smears frosting on his collar, joking with Mike like old friends.

It's loud, a little messy, and completely full.

And for the first time in a long time, so am I.

That's when it really hits me—just how deeply I've fallen for this man. Our letters have been a light in even the darkest days, our phone calls filled with laughter, teasing, and quiet promises of devotion. But this—seeing him so seamlessly folded into the rhythm of my family—it feels like the stamp on a letter that was already written. I love him. Wholly. Entirely. With every piece of my heart.

As we leave, I see it in his eyes. They're shimmering with something—it's hard to name. Not quite tears. Not quite longing. Just something full.

"Is everything all right?" I ask.

He's quiet for a moment before glancing over at me. "Yeah. I just... thank you. For bringing me here—to all of this. It means a lot to feel like part of a family again."

He pauses, then laughs nervously. "I mean—not that I am part of your family. I just meant... I don't know. This was nice."

I raise an eyebrow. "Mr. Madden, are you stammering?"

He grins. "A little, yeah. It's just—this was one of the happiest days I've had in a long time. Things with my family are... complicated. And after I lost my dad, I didn't think I'd feel that again. That sense of belonging."

He takes my hand gently. "Being with you? That's already top tier. But the package you come with—the people, the warmth, the crazy—it's something beautiful."

I squeeze his hand, heart still full from the day. "They liked you, you know."

He smiles, and for a moment, everything feels light.

Then I ask, quietly, "Does it bother you—doing things like this?"

His expression softens. "No. It just makes me wish I had anything close to it." He exhales slowly. "My mom and I... we never really had a relationship. My sister and I still write letters, but even that feels strained. Distant. We both saw too much, went through too much too young. I knew I needed to get out—that's why I joined the service. I needed purpose. But she stayed behind."

He looks out toward the streetlight, voice lower now. "When I got the telegram about my dad while I was deployed... I hated that I wasn't there. I think it shifted something in us. My mother, she was never a kind woman. And Katlin was left alone with her. Maybe I should've stayed. My dad could be difficult, sure—but he cared... in his own way."

He pauses, jaw tight, eyes distant.

"It was never like this though. There was no love baked into strudels. No warmth humming in the walls. You had to beg for it, like a starving child." He swallows. "Which we were, most of the time."

Then he lets out a small, strained laugh—like he's trying to lift the weight of it. "I mean, we weren't *actually* starving. It's just—things were hard. There was always yelling. Fighting. Doors slamming. Things breaking when they didn't need to. Would you believe I felt more at ease after I joined the Army?"

He glances at me, sheepish now. "Sorry. That got heavier than I meant."

I smile softly, then lean in and kiss him on the cheek. "Don't apologize," I say, my voice just above a whisper. "You don't have to carry it alone, you know."

He turns toward me, eyes searching mine—not with sadness, exactly, something quieter. Grateful, maybe. Or just seen.

I squeeze his hand. "You're allowed to have had a hard childhood *and* still deserve all of this."

He nods once. Then again, slower. "With you, it almost feels possible." He lets out a long sigh.

"We should go ice skating," he says abruptly. "Finish out your Christmas break strong."

"I love to skate," I say. "That sounds wonderful. Hopefully I don't hurt myself and have to explain bruises to the kids on Monday!"

"I'm sure you're perfectly graceful," he says, though the teasing smile on his face suggests he's picturing something else entirely.

"Tomorrow, then?" he asks.

"Tomorrow," I echo, nodding.

He leans in and kisses me—soft and certain—then pulls back with a smile that lingers.

"Goodnight, Miss Kirchberger."

And just like that, he turns and heads down the steps, leaving me standing in front of my apartment with cold hands and a warm heart.

I almost can't sleep—I'm so excited for our date. I decide today is a good day to rise with the sun. I'm awake anyway, might as well go look at something beautiful.

I wrap my hands around a mug of hot tea, the steam soft against my face, and pull my blanket tighter around my shoulders as I settle by the window. The sunrise feels like it's rewarding me for showing up. The sky spills pinks and oranges like a gift, and I take it all in, one slow breath at a time.

Okay. Three good things:

1. Yesterday was a wonderful day.
2. I'm so excited for my date today.
3. I am in love with Frank Madden.

As we step onto to the rink I take a quick look around, it's lit by soft golden bulbs strung overhead, casting lovely little halos on the ice. A radio hums out Elvis and the occasional crackle of static, I keep tying to focus to see if I can make out what song it is, but no luck. It's a Sunday evening, not too crowded, just a few teenagers clutching each other and an older couple gliding like they've been skating together for fifty years.

Frank wobbles beside me, arms out like a windmill. "I told you I have the grace of a drunken moose," he mutters. "You, however, seem to glide with the grace of a swan."

I laugh. "You're improving. Last lap you only almost fell twice, though if you notice I am purposefully leaving out the group of children taking their skating lesson that you took down like bowling pins."

"Progress, and yes thank you for not bringing it up otherwise my ego may have taken a serious hit," he says— just before catching the toe of his skate and stumbling directly into me.

We go down together in a tangle of limbs landing in a heap near the edge of the rink. My hat goes flying. Frank groans. "Well, that was dignified."

I'm laughing so hard I can barely breathe. "You took me down with you. You're a menace to society."

"You were in the blast zone," he says, grinning. "Collateral damage."

I reach for my hat and he reaches for my hand at the same time, and for a second, everything stills.

His glove presses to mine, and he's staring at me—blue eyes earnest, a little pink from the cold, a little winded. We're still sitting on the ice. My heart is pounding, and not from the fall.

"Trudy," he says, suddenly quiet. "You know I love you, right?"

It hangs there, suspended in the winter air between us.

I blink, breath catching. "Yeah," I whisper. "I do. And I love you too. I think I have for a while."

He exhales, like he's been holding it in for months. Maybe he has.

I squeeze his hand. "We're a mess, you know. We look ridiculous."

"Speak for yourself," he says. "I'm a professional, I should teach lessons—those kids may need a new instructor anyway, I think I took her out too."

I laugh again, leaning forward so our foreheads touch. "Kiss me before we freeze to the ice."

He does—gently at first, then deeper, until I forget how cold it is. The world around us blurs, and it's just the sound of our skates, the hiss of the wind, and the thrum of my heart beating against his.

When we finally stand, clumsy and flushed and happy, he brushes the snow from my coat. "You know this doesn't mean I'll get any better at skating."

"That's okay," I say, lacing my fingers through his. "You're already good at all the important stuff."

It was the perfect way to end my Christmas break.

Mrs. DeMarco had said that after Christmas break the school year tends to fly by—and she wasn't kidding. Before

I knew it, I was cutting out hearts for the February bulletin board.

I'm finally going to see Henry on Valentine's Day. After weeks of dodging him, I know I have to face him and end it properly. Valentine's feels like a cruel day to do it, but he didn't leave me much choice. He insisted he'd made the reservations weeks ago, his voice brimming with excitement, and I can't keep avoiding him forever, but I could certainly put it off until Valentine's Day.

The plan was simple enough: enjoy a nice dinner, let him have his evening, and then—after dessert—explain kindly that this isn't something I can continue. Surely, he'd understand. We've only ever been casual, after all. But the truth was that my feelings for Frank have grown far too strong to ignore.

Frank, on the other hand, asked to see me today, and I'm looking forward to it more than I care to admit. We've fallen into the habit of writing or calling nearly every day, and the thought of him has a way of brightening everything. He also asked if we could have a proper Valentine's dinner the Saturday after, since the holiday fell on a Friday this year—and he knew I'd be seeing Henry then, to finally put an end to things.

We met at a little coffee shop close to the school. The bell over the coffee shop door jingles as I step inside, still flushed from the chaos of the school day and the quick walk in the cold. Frank's already there, waving from a booth in the corner with two mugs of something steaming between them. He looks tired, but he always says the newsroom's worse on Fridays.

He looks at me, tired and a little embarrassed, something in my face must convince him though. He nods. Clearly trying to appease me.

I pay the bill with a hand that shakes more than I want to admit and we make our way to the doctor's office together—leaving our hot chocolates behind, the whipped cream already sinking under the weight of time.

Chapter 8

"Love does not consist in gazing at each other, but in looking outward together in the same direction." — Antoine de Saint-Exupéry

Non-Hodgkin lymphoma.

That's what the doctor said.

It's been two weeks since we first went in. They did a biopsy, ran some bloodwork, then sent us home to wait—with the weight of what it might be pressing on our chests.

And now we know.

Worst case scenario.

The words hang in the air like smoke, thick and cloying. My ears are still ringing. I feel untethered, like I'm floating just above the room, watching someone else in my place—someone gripping the arms of her chair like she might fall straight through the floor if she lets go.

"What does that mean, exactly?" I manage to ask, but my voice comes out dry and cracked. A whisper wrapped in sandpaper.

The doctor turns toward Frank, but Frank doesn't meet his eyes. He's staring straight ahead. Still. Quiet.

The doctor clears his throat and launches into something—something about lymph nodes, white blood cells, treatments, specialists. Words with sharp edges. Words that don't land because they're ricocheting off the inside of my skull.

I hear "*manageable.*"

I hear "*we caught it early.*"

I hear "*we'll talk options.*"

But all I can think is: *No. No. No. This isn't fair.* Not *him.* Not this.

I glance at Frank. His hands are folded in his lap, and I notice how tightly he's holding them together. Like if he lets go, he'll come apart. I reach for him and he holds my hand like a lifeline. I want to say something, to be brave for him.

But right now, all I can do is sit beside him and hope that's enough.

As we're standing up to leave, the doctor places a hand gently on my arm.

"Would you mind staying behind for just a moment?" he asks, nodding toward the hall.

Frank gives me a puzzled glance yet doesn't question it— just says he'll wait outside.

The door clicks shut behind him.

Then, the doctor looks at me—not unkindly, just with a distance that chills me more than the weather outside.

"You can still leave, you know," he says quietly. "You're young. If you want children someday... the radiation will take that chance away from you. This doesn't need to be your life. It's not easy. Get out now. He'll understand."

It takes me a full second to register what he's implying. Another to believe he actually said it.

I've never wanted to slap someone more in my life.

Instead, I stare at him and let the silence stretch.

"I didn't ask for your advice," I say, my voice low and steady. "And with all due respect, you can keep it."

I don't wait for a response. I open the door and step back into the hallway, where Frank is waiting. Still pale. Still quiet. But mine.

And I take his hand.

Because if this is going to be my life—then it's *mine* to choose.

Valentine's Day comes. Funny how the calendar keeps moving, even when you beg it to stay still. I know I can't cancel, so I go. I see Henry. My eyes are still a little swollen from crying, though it's been two days.

Frank said he needed a beat to take it all in, and I want to respect that. I told him I'd be seeing him Saturday though.

Everything shifted in that office. It's so clear now. And I don't want to waste another moment pretending otherwise: we belong with each other—for whatever time we're granted.

Henry's chosen another extravagant restaurant— showy, overdone, dripping in Valentine's decorations. I spot him across the room and run over.

He looks happy. And something else I can't quite place.

The waiter takes my coat, and I try to smooth my dress— navy with tiny hearts. I picked it because it didn't scream anything. Just... nice. Neutral. Safe.

Henry stands when he sees me. Smiles. He looks sharp, as always—charcoal blazer, cufflinks, hair combed just so.

"You look beautiful," he says, leaning in to kiss my cheek.

I murmur a thank you and take my seat, adjusting the cloth napkin on my lap mostly to avoid his eyes.

The table is drowning in red—roses, hearts, even the butter is shaped like cupids.

Small talk gets us through the appetizers. I nod, I smile.

He tells me a story about a client mix-up—something about the wrong file—and I do my best to laugh in the right places.

But I feel like a ghost version of myself.

Then dessert comes, and with it, a silver tray. The waiter sets it down with a bit too much flourish. There's a box on it.

I blink. "What's that?"

Henry grins. "Go on. Open it."

I hesitate. I know what it is before I touch it. My heart drops into my stomach. I open the box anyway. A ring. Elegant. Traditional. It catches the light in that calculated way rings do in department store ads.

I don't say anything.

Henry clears his throat and straightens in his chair.

"I spoke to your father," he says. "He gave his blessing. Actually, more than that—he said he couldn't imagine a better match for you." He smiles, proud. "I agree."

I close the box gently.

"Henry," I say softly. "I can't."

His expression flickers, then firms. "Trudy... I've been thinking about this for a while. I know we haven't made anything official, not in so many words, but I think we both feel it."

I blink.

"We haven't even gone steady," I whisper. He laughs— lightly, dismissively. Like I've said something sweet and silly.

"Of course, you're overwhelmed," he says, reaching for my hand. "That's why I'm not expecting an answer tonight. Just think about it."

I want to pull my hand away. It feels acidic.

Instead, I shake my head—small, certain. "No."

He doesn't acknowledge it. Just turns back to his dessert, as if the evening is still going according to plan.

I stare down at the unopened menu. The ring is still sitting there. And I can feel it, even with my eyes closed—glinting like a warning. All around us, people are laughing, sipping wine, clinking glasses. Everyone's enjoying their dinners. And I feel like I'm suffocating.

I need to talk to Dad.

When he gets on the phone, I can hear the warmth in his voice. He thinks I'm calling to thank him.

"Hey sweetheart," he says. "Quite a surprise, huh?"

"How could you do this?" I snap.

"What?"

"Make this decision for me."

There's a pause. "He's smart, he has a good job, he makes good money. You'll have a good life with him. I don't understand why you're so angry."

"Dad, I'm almost 27 years old. You don't think I can make this decision for myself?"

"He asked for my blessing, and I gave it."

"Well, *un*-give it!"

"No." His voice is firm. "I stand by it. I think he's a good match for you, Trudy. You'll be taken care of."

There it is. I feel the words before I say them.

"That's what you really think, isn't it? That I can't take care of myself. You've never thought I could."

"You're a young woman in a tough world—why not let someone take care of you? Is that so wrong to want for you?"

I can hear the strain in his voice now, more fear than anger.

"I've lived with *nothing*. I watched the German Mark collapse. I came here with *nothing* and found work during the Depression—just to give you the life you have, the life you want. You don't know, Trudy. It can all happen again! He'll provide for you. You could have a good life. A comfortable life."

"These are *my* decisions to make."

I know some of the anger in my voice isn't just about him.

169

"You're not thinking straight, Trudy. You're getting older, and you're still not married—You're a smart girl, but sometimes you let your feelings get the better of you."

It's everything—Frank, the proposal, the fear, the grief, what my dad said—bleeding into this moment, spilling over where it doesn't quite belong.

And I know it isn't fair.

But I'm angry.

And I'm tired.

And I'm sad.

And right now, I just need that to be okay.

"Let me talk to Mom," I say, my voice breaking.

There's a beat, then—

"Trud-a-la, my love, what's happened?"

That's all it takes.

I break. I cry. And she just listens. Doesn't interrupt. Doesn't try to fix it. Just stays. After we hang up, I sit on my couch and cry.

I cry for the life I thought I'd have.

I cry over the argument with my father.

I cry for the inevitable fight still waiting with Henry.

I cry for the grief I know is coming.

I cry for the children I may never have.

I cry for Frank—and whatever he might be feeling, wherever he is.

I cry and cry and cry.

I give myself this time to grieve. I give myself tonight. Because when the sun rises tomorrow, I'll need to be strong—for Frank, yes, but for myself too. He'll be carrying so much, and I need to remind him: there is still joy in the day. There are colors in the sunset, laughter to be found. We have time together. And we can't waste it on silly things like sadness.

With the rising of the sun on Saturday, I know what I have to do.

My face is still swollen, my eyes rimmed red, but there's a quiet determination stirring in me now. I will move forward. There's beauty in fleeting things. We can find joy in the small moments and figure out the big ones later.

As long as there's Frank, we'll find a way forward.

The air is cold—so cold I feel it deep in my bones as I swing my legs out of bed. I make myself a cup of tea. It's still dark out, but I carry it onto the balcony anyway. I decide to watch the sunrise.

I sit there, wrapped in a blanket, watching the steam swirl and disappear into the morning air. The grief settles into me—not as a wave this time, but something quieter.

Something that's found a home inside me. But it's different now. It's laced with something else—a glimmer of hope, faint but steady, like the first light breaking through the clouds.

Find three good things, I remind myself.

1. These colors are beautiful. I bet Frank would want to paint them.

2. My tea is warm and soothing.

3. I get to see Frank later.

There. That's the first step. I can do this. For Frank... and for me too.

Frank had originally planned a nice romantic dinner, but I don't think either of us is up for anything big.

I called him and invited him over instead—told him we'd order Chinese food and keep it simple. He sounded hesitant, unsure about doing anything at all. But after a pause, he agreed. Reluctantly, but he agreed.

I ran out quickly to the store and grabbed some Valentine's decorations—everything was half-off anyway, being the day after. By the time I'm done, the apartment looks like St. Valentine himself threw up in here.

I'm determined to make it festive and fun.

I light a few candles to give the room a soft, romantic glow. Then, just because I can't help myself, I put on a ridiculous headband with two glittery hearts on springs. They bounce with every step I take, tilting at odd angles like they're drunk or dizzy or maybe just in love.

The Chinese food arrives earlier than expected, and I set it all out on the kitchen table.

I open the boxes, fluff the rice with a fork, and arrange everything just so—plates stacked, chopsticks laid out, the good napkins for once.

It's nothing fancy, but I want it to feel like something. Something easy. Something comforting. Something we can just sit down and dive into—no pressure, no pretense. Just us.

I watch the clock like a hawk, nervous he won't show. Each minute stretches longer than the last. But then—a knock at the door.

There he is. And just like that, my world fills with color again. I'm breathing again. We can get through this.

He steps inside, takes in the room—the candles, the scattered hearts, the absurd headband bobbing on my head—and he laughs. A real laugh. Not a polite one. Not one just to make me feel better. A real, from-the-belly, spark-is-still-in-there kind of laugh.

You like?" I ask, doing a little twirl to show off my red dress, my ridiculous headband, and the wildly decorated apartment.

"I love," he says. But his voice is soft. And there's a sadness in it that catches me off guard.

"And the main course—only the finest for you, Frank." I gesture grandly to the kitchen table.

He smiles but it doesn't quite reach his eyes.

I exhale, long and deep. The show is over.

"Okay," I say quietly. "Let's just get to it then."

"Okay," he says quietly. "This—being with you—has been the best thing that's ever happened to me."

I see tears brimming in his eyes.

"Things haven't always made sense in my life. But you came into it like a tornado, and it woke me up. And I'll always be grateful for that."

I look at him for a long beat and blink a few times.

"What are you trying to say, Frank?"

He swallows hard.

"You can't want to stay with me... not after what that doctor said. After what we learned."

"Why give a bird wings if you're not going to let them fly?" I ask softly. "Why give women a brain if you don't want them to think for *themselves*, Frank?"

"I do. I *do* want that. I just..." He exhales shakily. "You won't be able to have kids, Trudy. I won't be able to give you that. Even if the radiation doesn't eliminate that chance completely, how can I make that choice knowing

174

this is looming?" He pauses, voice quieter now. "I wouldn't want to do that to a child. I know what it feels like to lose a father, and I couldn't choose that for someone else."

"I know."

"We don't know how long I have."

"I know."

We hold each other's gaze.

"The food's getting cold, let's eat." I take his hand and lead him to the table.

We sit at the table, lit by candlelight, with the weight of everything pulling up its own chair beside us.

We don't speak right away.

But slowly, I see him start to thaw. His shoulders ease, his jaw unclenches. He relaxes into the easy rhythm we've always had, and I feel him—really feel him—coming back to me.

"Trudy," he says softly, "I mean it… if this is all too much for you, it's okay. I won't have any hard feelings. You can leave."

"You sound like that doctor."

"What?"

"Nothing. But I'll tell you—I have a few choice words I'd love to say to him. Maybe I'll write him a letter."

Frank huffs a laugh. "I'm sure he thought he was being helpful."

"Besides, if I wanted something different," I say, grabbing a dumpling, "I could always accept Henry's marriage proposal."

Frank freezes. "Henry's *what?*"

"Henry proposed."

He blinks. "You should say yes."

I squint at him. "*Now* you sound like my father."

"Well, he's a smart man."

"Don't you *start*. I don't want Henry." I point my chopsticks at him. "I want you, *dummy*."

He doesn't say anything right away.

But his hand finds mine across the table. A quiet, steady touch. His thumb brushes over my knuckles, and I feel something loosen in my chest.

"This is what I want too," he says softly. "In case I haven't said it. And thank you—for today. It's... everything. But if you don't... if you want to think about all this—take a day or two. Let it settle."

"No." I say, firmly. "Why does everyone think I don't know my own mind?"

I pull my hand back just slightly—not to push him away, but to hold my own ground.

"I don't want time to think. I don't want space. I don't want to waste another minute without you. Don't you get that?"

I take a deep breath, trying to tamp down the sudden heat in my chest.

"If this is the time we have—if this is the time you have—why would we squander it?"

I pause, suddenly unsure. My voice softens.

"Unless…" I glance at him. "Unless you don't want to be with me?"

He laughs—genuine, warm.

"Of course I do. I just don't want to drag you through the inevitable pain. This isn't going to be easy, and I don't want that for you. I want to be with you. But I also want you to be *happy*."

"Well, that's easy—because you make me happy."

"Will you just take one day? Just one day to think it over? I know you *know* your own mind, I'm not questioning that. But really think about what this life might be."

"If I *say* I will, will you let this go?" Rolling my eyes.

"Yes."

"Okay then," I say, sitting up straighter. "Good. It's settled." I wave my chopsticks for emphasis. "So enough of this crazy talk."

He smiles—so warmly it could bring summer early.

"Okay," he says, voice lighter now. "Enough crazy talk." He lifts his glass. "Let's celebrate Valentine's Day."

The rest of dinner passes without a hitch, and I can see his spirits start to lift. By the time we got to dessert, a strawberry shortcake and two spoons, my Frank is nearly back. The weight of the news still sat on his shoulders, but he's cracking jokes with ease again, and I feel that tight spot in my chest loosen—just a little.

We laugh and tease each other, slipping back into something familiar. When he says he's tired, I don't argue. I walk him to the door to say goodnight.

He holds my gaze, serious for just a moment. I can tell he wants to kiss me goodnight—but he is giving me time.

Instead, he takes my hand and presses a soft kiss to it.

"Goodnight, Trudy. Don't forget to write."

So I do.

After he leaves, I sit down at the table.

It's still covered in decorations and dinner crumbs, the candles flickering low.

But I have a lot I need to say—things that can't wait. Things that only paper will let me say right.

Dear Frank,

I know I said I'd think about it. But let's be honest——when have I ever waited to say what's on my mind?

I've been sitting here at the table——still wearing that ridiculous headband, by the way——and all I can think is: what exactly am I supposed to be thinking about?

Whether I want to be with you? I already know the answer. I've known it for a long time, longer than I'd let myself admit out loud. I know you're scared. I am too. And yes, your diagnosis changes some things. But not the important ones.

Not how I feel about you.

Not how I see you.

Not how much I want to be with you for as long as I get to.

You said I could walk away. That you'd understand.

But let me be clear: _I don't want to_.

Why would I choose to be sad without you when I could be laughing with you instead? Why spend our time crying apart when we could be together, even if we're still figuring it all out?

You're it for me, Frank. That's not something I need to think over. So if you're waiting for me to make up my mind—consider this my official declaration. I want you. Just as you are. And I'm not going anywhere.

P.S. I saved you a fortune cookie, but I ate your egg roll. Even true love has limits.

Love,

Trudy

I reread the letter three times before sealing it. My mind is made, and my path is clear. Everyone else will just have to get on board. There's a strange kind of peace in knowing your choice—in no longer wondering which way to go, just... walking toward it.

On Sunday, I wake up again at sunrise.

It's freezing, but I know I need these quiet moments. They're helping with the grief. I allow myself the time— not a lot, just enough to let the sadness rise and slip out into the air.

I don't want it trapped inside, rattling around in my head. Grief can do that. Sadness can echo and multiply until your mind becomes a chamber of pain. So rather than let it stick, I let it go—let it fly free with the cooing pigeons, high into the morning sky, until it disappears into the clouds.

I promised Frank I'd "think about what this life would be."

And all I can imagine are mornings together, looking at each other over coffee mugs, laughing over pancakes drizzled in syrup.

I imagine us traveling the world.

I imagine treating my nieces and nephew like they're our own—and maybe that will feel like enough.

I imagine Christmas mornings full of laughter, New Year's Eve kisses, birthday cakes being cut with candles still flickering.

And the more I think, the clearer the images become.

And the clearer they become, the more I ache for it.

Silly Frank. I think when he asked me to really consider our future, he thought I might walk away. But all it's done is solidify how much I want it.

How much I want *him.*

If anything, thinking about our time together has only made me want more of it.

Chapter 9

"Two roads diverged in a wood, and I— I took the one less traveled by." —
Robert Frost

By Monday morning, I'm back at school.

The pigeons and sunrise are gone—replaced by the clatter of lunchboxes, the squeak of shoes on linoleum, the chorus of "Miss Kirchberger! Miss Kirchberger!" echoing down the hall.

It's strange, holding so much inside and still smiling like everything's fine. Like my world isn't quietly rearranging itself in the background.

I move through the day with practiced ease—math worksheets, reading groups, correcting pencil grips, gently redirecting whispered chatter.

But underneath it all, I'm wrestling. And they'd never know.

They see their happy teacher, the one who corrects their grammar and fixes their ponytails without missing a beat.

But I'm wrestling with the ache of my father's disappointment. Wrestling with the fight I know is coming with Henry. Wrestling with the ache in my chest when I think of Frank—of our dinner, of what comes next. And still, I show up. For them. For myself. Because someone has to make sure Teddy doesn't glue his elbow to the desk again.

Mrs. DeMarco asked me—innocently, casually—if I did anything fun for Valentine's Day.

And just like that, it all came rushing back.

The restaurant.

The ring.

Oh God, the ring.

The proposal.

The call with my father.

"It depends what you mean by fun," I say, too brightly.

She raises her eyebrows—curious. Waiting.

I give her a tight smile, the kind that says *please don't press.*

"Let's just say it was eventful."

She lightly touches my arm. "This job... it pulls a lot out of a person," she says gently. "If you ever need to talk— about anything non-curriculum related—I hope you know you can come to me."

I place my hand over hers, feeling my throat tighten at the kindness, the simple human connection.

Get it together, Trudy.

"Thank you," I manage. "I may take you up on that—once things settle down a bit."

She smiles and nods, and without another word, walks back to her classroom.

When I get home, I call Frank. He doesn't answer.

I busy myself with little things around the apartment—some cleaning here, a few dishes there. Then I decide to call my mom.

The phone rings, and my dad answers. I hang up.

Childish? Absolutely.

But I'm not ready to talk to him.

I call again. He picks up on the first ring. I hang up again.

I call a third time, and he answers—clearly annoyed. I sigh, tired of my own game.

"Put Mom on, please."

"Trudy?" he says.

"Please put Mom on," I repeat, flat and sharp.

"Don't be like this, mein *liebling*."

"I'll be whatever *I choose*."

It comes out too harsh. He doesn't deserve it.

I know that.

But I'm so angry.

And even though I know he shouldn't be the vessel for all of it, the anger keeps funneling straight through him.

He sighs. Deep and heavy. There's sadness in it, and it annoys me—which only aggravates me more.

Because I know this isn't all his fault.

But I didn't inherit my stubbornness from the thin air, I suppose.

I hear the phone being passed over.

"Hello, my love..." my mom says gently.

"Hi, Mom."

"Are you feeling a little better today?"

"A bit. Things are hard, but I'm managing."

There's a pause. Then—

"Then I'm going to ask you to go easier on your father. He's trying. He loves you. He didn't mean to hurt you. He thought he was helping. He just wants you safe and protected. That's a father's job, after all. You'll understand when you're a parent."

I pause, gripping the phone a little tighter. *But I won't be a parent.* It stings deep in places I didn't know existed. But if not having children means more time with Frank, that choice is clear—to me at least.

"I'm not a child, Mom," I say. My voice is calm, but it's colder than I mean for it to be. "I don't need to be protected. Especially not from someone I love."

She doesn't say anything right away.

"I know you think he means well," I continue, "but that doesn't mean it didn't hurt. You don't get to hide behind good intentions forever. At some point, it's about impact."

There's a quiet breath on the other end. Then:

"He's *trying*, Trudy."

"Well, I'm tired of trying to make excuses for him."

My voice cracks just slightly, and I hate that it does.

"I know you love him. I do too. Things are just a little *intense* right now. We just… need time to cool off."

A pause.

"Okay," she says gently. "Was there something you were calling about, then?"

I sigh, unsure of how to move forward. I was going to tell her about Frank. About how I feel. About what happened with the doctor. But it doesn't feel right anymore. Like a small string starting to fray at the edges—too loose, too fragile to tug on right now.

"I just wanted to say hi," I say quietly. "And I know things were tense the other night. But... I love you."

"I love you too. We'll speak soon, my love."

I hang up the phone like it's made of glass, as fragile as the relationship is starting to feel.

I still feel unsettled, so I make one more call.

Mike answers on the fourth ring.

He barely gets his "hello" out before I'm off...

"You remember Frank?"

A pause. "You mean your *friend*? Helped you move in, came to Denise's party—yeah, I remember him. The guy who held Karen's thermos for an hour like it was his job?" The way he says friend makes it very clear, I hadn't been fooling anyone, not even myself. He was always more than that, even if I wasn't ready to admit it out loud then.

I smile despite myself. "That's the one."

"I remember thinking he had a good head on his shoulders. And a soft spot for kids. He painted a nice sign too. Why?"

"Because it's him," I say, barely above a whisper. "It's always been *him*."

Mike doesn't say anything right away, but I hear the smile in his voice when he finally speaks. "Took you long enough."

I let out a quiet laugh and sank back against the cushions. "It's not that simple."

"It never is, is it?"

"I haven't told Mom and Dad. Especially Dad. He's still holding out hope for Henry."

"Hmm."

"And it's not just that. He's sick. Non-Hodgkin lymphoma. He told me recently."

Mike goes quiet. "That's a lot."

"I know."

I hesitate, then blurt it all out in one breath. "Henry proposed."

Silence.

"Wow."

"Yeah."

"And... you said?"

"No! *Obviously* not! We weren't even going steady. He must've slammed his head on his diamond-encrusted wallet if he even thought I'd say yes. But he just ignored me and kept eating dessert like I hadn't said anything." I sigh. "Dad gave his blessing—*and then some*—and we got into a big fight, and now I just don't know anything anymore."

Mike exhales slowly. "Trudy... I saw the way Frank looked at you at the party. And the way you looked at him when you thought no one was watching. I haven't seen that in you before."

I blink fast. "I'm scared."

"Of what?"

"Of Dad's reaction. Of losing someone I just found."

There's a pause. Then: "You might. But if you walk away now, you'll lose him anyway. And not because of cancer—because of fear. And that's not you, Trudy."

I breathe in slow. "I needed to hear that."

"Listen, I've got your back," Mike says. "You don't have to rush with Dad. But when you do tell him—whatever happens—you've got me.

"Either way, Trudy, you can't say yes to a marriage proposal from someone you don't see yourself with. Marriage is for life. So, ask yourself—who would you want for life? If it's not Henry, then... the answer's already obvious. And listen, Dad just wants you safe. That's all this is. Try not to be too mad at him. He's not trying to hurt

189

you—he's doing what he thinks is right. You're being a little hard on him. I know you've got a lot on your plate, but just… try to look at the whole picture."

"Thanks, Mike. I know. I'm just… mad. And upset."

"Anytime. Okay, I should go—it sounds like the kids are redecorating the wallpaper with the brownies Annette just made."

"Well, you can't say they aren't artistic."

"I would never. But I will say they're about to be in trouble."

I hang up and laugh, picturing the chaos unfolding at their house—brownie smeared across the walls, one or all of the kids proudly showing off their masterpiece, blissfully unaware they've done anything wrong.

So innocent. And it stings, bittersweet, right in the center of my chest.

Over the next few days, Henry calls every day. And every day, I tell him the same thing: Either stop calling or just accept that the answer is *no*.

He laughs each time, like I'm being precious.

"You're sweet, Trudy. But you don't know what's best for you."

"Two hot chocolates?" I ask, smiling as I slide into the booth.

"I figured you needed a reward," he says. "And I needed sugar, but seeing you may satisfy my sweet fix."

We settle in easily—talking about our days, the kids, the headline he's chasing. His hand brushes mine once across the table, and I pretend not to notice how my heart stutters. That's when something shifts.

He brings a napkin to his nose. Clears his throat. Then again.

I pause mid-sentence. "Are you okay?"

He nods but doesn't speak—just leans forward a little. And then I see it. Blood. A slow trickle from his nose, seeping through the napkin. He pinches the bridge and tilts forward, clearly trying to play it off.

"It's fine," he mumbles. "Just dry air, maybe. You know how it gets in the winter."

But it doesn't stop. Five minutes pass, then ten. The napkin is soaked and his hot chocolate's gone cold. My own stomach is twisting.

"Frank," I say softly, "we should go. Let's just get you looked at."

"It's just a nosebleed. I saw way worse in Korea."

"It's not *just*. And you're not talking me out of this."

I want to reach through the phone and flick him on the forehead.

If there was ever a moment I knew this wasn't the life meant for me, that sentence alone would've done it.

That—and Frank's eyes.

The curve of his smile.

The way his arms flex when he paints.

And the way my cheeks heat when he looks at me.

And the way he really sees me—not the idea of me, but *me*.

It's been about a month of dodging Henry, and I finally decide I need to give him the ring back.

He had insisted I take it—convinced I was saying yes. I wasn't. I never was.

Now I'm waiting in the park for Henry, the ring box burning a hole in my pocket.

My mind, though, is somewhere else entirely.

Frank has started radiation therapy. The doctors seem relatively optimistic—said it looked *slow-growing*, that we'd caught it early.

We're hopeful. We have a plan. We're moving forward— and moving forward together.

He doesn't like me coming to his radiation appointments. Not yet, at least.

They only lasted about a half hour, and he goes his way home from work, always saying it doesn't bother him all that much.

Once, when I asked how it went, he shrugged and said, "Not bad. I get to lie down while they microwave me. It's practically a spa day."

Then he laughed like it was nothing. He smoothed my hair and told me not to worry.

"Try not to worry, my love. No one makes it out of this life alive—let's enjoy it while we can."

Then he laughed again, and kissed me like we had all the time in the world. And I let him.

But I've seen it. It's starting to make him a little more tired than usual.

I'm so wrapped in my thoughts I don't even see Henry approaching. When I finally noticed him, I stand—determined to keep this quick and clean.

He smiles lazily when he sees me, then leans in to kiss my cheek.

This guy. Where does he get the audacity? Does he manufacture it himself?

I take a half-step back before he can try anything more.

"Hi," I say flatly.

"Hi yourself." He grins, like this is a date. Like I didn't ask him here to return an engagement ring he gave me without asking.

I pull the ring box from my coat pocket and hold it out to him. "Here."

He blinks. "What's this?"

"The ring, Henry."

He doesn't move to take it. "Trudy, come on."

"I'm not marrying you."

He scoffs, still smiling like it's a game. "You're being emotional."

And there it is.

"No," I say, my voice rising. "I'm being honest. I told you I needed time. You ignored me. You bulldozed right past what I wanted and handed me a ring like I was supposed to be grateful."

"You don't know what you want."

"Don't you *dare*," I snap. "I may not have everything figured out, but I know this isn't it. I don't want a life that's been picked out for me like a dress off a rack."

He finally frowns. "So this is about that other guy."

A beat.

"He can't give you a future. People talk—he's a ticking clock, Trudy." He says it gently, like he's offering wisdom. Like he's doing me a favor.

Something in me *snaps*. I don't know where he heard about Frank, and honestly I don't care. Because this was never about him.

"This is about *me*." I press the ring box into his hand. "You gave this to the version of me you imagined. The quiet little wife who'd smile politely at dinner parties and keep her opinions to herself."

I step back, breath sharp in my throat. "And for the record? I'd rather have five minutes with someone who sees me than a lifetime with someone who doesn't."

"You're being unfair."

"Maybe. But hopefully I'm finally being *clear*."

He stares at me, waiting for me to take it back. I don't.

Then he looks at me and smiles in that infuriating way of his—calm, smug, untouchable.

"You'll come to your senses in a few weeks," he says. "I'll give you time."

And that's when I know—really know—I'm done.

I turn and walk away, heart pounding, cheeks burning—but lighter than I've felt in weeks.

Chapter 10

"The secret of staying young is to live honestly, eat slowly, and lie about your age."
— *Lucille Ball*

It's hard to believe it's already my birthday, March has snuck up on me in a way I wasn't expecting. Frank wanted to do something fun, but with the radiation I can tell he's more tired than he's letting on. The circles under his eyes are darker this week, and he's been sitting more, even when he says he's fine.

"How about just something small," I say.

"Or something huge," he counters, lifting an eyebrow.

"Or tiny," I toss back.

"Or gigantic."

I look at him, amused.

I don't need something huge for my birthday. I'm turning twenty-seven, not *seven*.

"We'll see," he says with a conspiratorial grin

When my birthday does arrive, Frank picks me up and says he's taking me for a drive. It's a Saturday and I assume we're going to a drive-in, or maybe a dinner.

The longer we're in the car, the more familiar the route becomes—Long Island. And not just anywhere. My brother's house.

"Are we going to Mike's?" I ask, squinting out the window.

"Who?" he says, raising a brow without looking away from the road.

"Frank…" I start, laughing. "What did you do?"

"I have no idea what you're talking about," he says—grinning now, trying (and failing) to keep a straight face.

We pull up, and kids are already spilling out of the house.

They must've seen Dad's white van—because it's not just my nieces and nephew anymore. All the neighborhood kids have come running, swarming like they know there's something special in the air.

The idea of seeing my dad makes me feel something complicated—nervous and happy all at once.

Like I *am* seven again and also twenty-seven, all in the same breath.

Frank glances at me and shrugs like, *oops, guess the secret's out.* I laugh, but my heart's already beating faster.

As we walk up the path, I spot Mike in the doorway grinning like he's ten and just pulled off the world's best prank.

Inside, it smells like lemon cake and too many bodies in one space. I'm wrapped in hugs before I can even get my coat off—Theresa clinging to my waist, Karen jumping up and down yelling "Happy birthday!" Michael Jr. trying to act cool but clearly thrilled I'm here.

Out of the corner of my eye, I spot Caroline and Patty weaving their way through the crowd, pretending they're not about to ambush me with hugs—but their faces give them away. They're both wearing ridiculous party hats, and I can imagine Caroline plopping it on Patty's head demanding she look festive before I get here.

And then, from the back of the room, I hear it.

"Trud-a-la?"

I turn, and there they are.

My parents. Standing just beyond the back door, half-lit in the late afternoon sun. Mom in her best cardigan, eyes already welling up. And Dad—holding a pie dish like it's a peace offering.

He looks sheepish. Proud. Nervous. He's the one who steps forward first.

"I told your mother I wasn't going to cry," he says, clearing his throat. "So we'll pretend this is just dust in my eye."

I laugh, even as my throat tightens. "Pie dust?"

"Very potent kind," he nods. "Apple."

And then he opens his arms. I don't hesitate.

"Happy birthday," he says softly.

I spot Annette zig-zagging through the guests, making sure everything's in order. I make a point to seek her out—thank her for hosting, maybe give her a minute to breathe. It couldn't have been easy getting everything together, but she says she was genuinely happy to do it.

She's beaming today, and I don't want to pry—but Annette dives in anyway, sharing that she has a slight lead on her natural mother.

Apparently, a cousin told her it wasn't a formal adoption after all. She was left with someone her natural mother trusted, which means there won't be any paper trail to follow.

It's the first real whiff of anything. And while I think I would've found that discouraging—having even less to go on—it seems to lift her spirits. And honestly? That's enough for me to be happy too.

The party moves around us—people filtering in and out, laughter rising and fading like waves.

Eventually, I find myself across the room, mid-laugh with Patty, when something over her shoulder catches my eye.

Across the room, by the far window, I see them—Frank and my dad, standing close enough to talk but far enough from the crowd that no one else seems to notice.

At first, it makes me smile. There's something quietly miraculous about seeing them in the same frame—some of the most important men in my life, side by side, talking like they might actually have something in common.

But the longer I watch, the more my smile fades.

Dad's talking with his hands—too much. His gestures are sharp, animated, bordering on dramatic.

And Frank... Frank isn't smiling. He's standing straight as a board, nodding a little too slowly. I see it—the stiffening in his shoulders, the way his jaw tightens just slightly.

Whatever this conversation is, it's not a good one.

And suddenly the room feels too warm, the lights too bright, the noise too loud.

Patty says something I know is supposed to be a punchline—something about the guy she went on a date with yesterday—but I don't catch it. I laugh politely anyway.

"You okay?" she asks, her voice softening. "Feels like you're a million miles away all of a sudden."

"Yes—yes, I'm so sorry," I say quickly. "I just noticed something I have to take care of."

"That's okay—it's your birthday." She smiles. "But I'm retelling that story later, because it's a doozy."

I smile, and my heart warms.

Everyone should have friends like these.

I weave through the crowd toward the window, where Frank and my dad are still talking. But Frank sees me coming, and just like that—the conversation ends. He straightens a little, gives my dad a brief nod.

"Everything okay over here, boys?" I ask, sliding into my lightest tone. "Are we playing nice?"

"We were debating pie flavors. It got intense," Frank says, his tone dry, his smile thin.

"Well," I reply, matching his tone but watching both of their faces, "you know how we feel about our pies. I wouldn't challenge him on it."

My dad chuckles—just once—but it sounds more like a cough. Frank doesn't say anything more, and I feel the air shift, just slightly.

"I wouldn't dream of it," he says after a beat. "Speaking of—I hear there's a killer apple pie somewhere. Let's go grab a slice."

He places a hand on my back, gentle but sure, guiding me toward the dessert table.

I let him lead me. But as we walk, I glance back over my shoulder. My father's still standing there, arms crossed, his expression tight. Worried, angry and a little sad, balled into one. Whatever they were talking about, it's still clinging to him. And it definitely wasn't pie.

When we're at the dessert table, I try to ask him what that was about—whatever he and my dad were discussing—but he swats me away gently and hands me a slice of pie.

"Nothing to worry over, darling."

Then, with zero warning, he twirls me and dips me so dramatically I burst out laughing, already forgetting what I was trying to ask in the first place.

"Thank you for planning this," I say once I've caught my breath. "I don't know how much was you and how much was them—" I nod toward Mike and Annette, both pretending not to watch us— "but either way. Thank you."

His eyes soften.

"Of course. It's your birthday. And I, for one, am very glad you were born."

Then his tone shifts—just slightly—but enough that I know something else is coming.

"Speaking of," he adds, "I have a very small gift I'd like to give you."

He walks me over to the pile of presents and immediately pulls his out. It's wrapped in newspaper, the funny pages facing out. He hands it to me with a proud little grin.

I open it carefully. Inside is a small leather-bound notebook and a fountain pen.

He's smiling so wildly I can't help but smile back.

"This way," he says, "no matter where you are, you can write down what you're thinking. You'll never forget to write. You'll never forget what you want to write about."

He pauses, just for a breath. "And I want to hear about it all, Trudy. I love that mind of yours—and hearing what you're thinking, it's... it's wonderful."

He glances down, almost shy for a second. "I love your letters. Never stop writing to me."

His voice is softer now, like he's not sure if he meant to say it all out loud. "They're such a bright spot for me. I bring them with me sometimes when... well—"

He clears his throat. "I just have them with me. When I need something to distract myself."

He's laughing now, aware he's rambling. "So I guess this is really a gift for me too."

"It's perfect," I say, not realizing until the words are out just how true they are.

We drive home in the kind of silence that only happens when nothing needs to be said—and when you're finally with someone who lets you be exactly who you are.

The roads are mostly empty, the glow of streetlights flicker across Frank's face as he drives—one hand on the wheel, the other resting between us. I watch the way his fingers tap softly against his thigh, like he's still holding the rhythm of the night.

I think about the pie, the laughter, the kids, my mother's cardigan, my father's eyes when he hugged me then his too-tight smile. I think about the way Frank dipped me by the dessert table, how the world tilted just enough to make me laugh. And I think about the notebook, still resting in my lap, like a promise I hadn't known I was waiting for.

The night was messy. Lovely. Imperfect. Real. And somewhere between the cake and the quiet goodbyes, I felt it. This life—whatever it is we're building—it's not safe or certain or neat.

As it turns out, I don't need safe or neat, after all. Maybe this is what I didn't know I always needed. It's more than I could have imagined.

Frank glances over at me at a red light, eyebrows raised just slightly. I smile at him in the soft glow of the traffic light and reach for his hand, bringing it into my lap. With a deep sigh, I look out the window. This feeling—It's the kind I want to bottle up and keep forever. Just me and this man, driving home from a family I love. And in this moment, everything feels steady—even if just for a little while.

I close my eyes for a second and wish I could press this feeling between the pages of my new notebook—just to keep it a little longer.

We finally made it to Easter break.

Life's been a blur lately—a mix of paperwork, lesson plans, and Frank's doctor's appointments. He still doesn't let me come with him, but he calls me every day afterward.

Always with a joke. Always trying to make it sound like it's no big deal.

Frank said he wanted to go out to eat on Friday. It's Good Friday, so we'll find somewhere close—nothing that requires too much walking—and somewhere we can get a vegetarian option. No meat on Fridays. Especially not Good Friday.

He sounds excited, and I don't ask why. I just want to hold onto whatever gave him that extra pep in his voice.

I find us a booth and place the order. I spot the Coca-Cola on the shelf but leave it there. I gave it up for Lent. Just two more days—I promised myself I'd wait until Easter. So, water for me, a Coke for Frank, and two slices each.

He looks tired, but his eyes are bright. There's something buzzing beneath the surface.

He kisses me right on the lips the second he sees me.

"Hi, Trudy."

"Well, hello to you too."

We pick the pizza place from our first real date. It's cute, close, and carries a kind of comfort. A good omen, maybe.

"So that's it," Frank says as we sit down, exhaling like he's been holding his breath for weeks. "No more zapping."

I smile, but I'm watching him closely. "How do you feel?"

"Like I ran a marathon with my bones on backwards," he says, grinning. Then softer: "Like I'm lucky. The doctor says this is it for a while now, just monthly checks, and if I notice anything at home to come in. But the radiation seemed to do something. It's not gone obviously, but..." He trails off, then looks at me tenderly. "I really am so lucky."

He reaches into his coat pocket and pulls out a small box. My heart skips.

"You're not serious."

"Dead serious," he says. "And very much alive. So let's do something reckless and wonderful."

I open the box. The ring is breathtaking—simple, but striking. A diamond in the center, with a sapphire on either side. Blue like his eyes. Like mine too, set together forever.

I can't help the thought that comes rushing in, uninvited but insistent: My dad will be so happy. I'm finally getting married.

I look up from the ring. My eyes are wet, though I don't remember crying.

Frank's moving now—getting down on one knee right there in the booth, like it's the most natural thing in the world.

"Marry me, Trudy. *Please*."

"Of course," I breathe. "Yes. Of course."

I take his face in my hands and kiss him—soft, certain, joyful.

I pull away and look at his face. I take it all in—memorizing every detail of this moment, imprinting it like a photograph I never want to lose. The deep blue of his eyes. The light brown of his coat. The curve of his smile. The smell of the pizzeria—warm, familiar, comforting. The feel of his stubble under my fingertips. All of it.

He slips the ring onto my finger and slides back into the booth just as our pizza arrives.

Life around us continues. Ours—forever changed. Forever linked over two slices. The thought is so comforting, I want to swim in it. Float in it. Stay here forever.

I glance at the ring, then back at him.

"What did my father say?" I ask softly. "I know you asked. You may not be a traditional man, but I know you hold some sentimentality."

He shifts, visibly uncomfortable. "Ah. Well. He said no."

I blink. "What?"

"He wouldn't give his blessing," Frank says. "Or his permission...or anything really. But I figured... that's a formality anyway. For a minute, I thought about not asking you at all after. But then I thought—hell, you're an adult. You can make your own choices."

"He said no," I repeat, slower this time, like the words are heavy in my mouth.

"Yes," Frank says quietly. "I'm sorry."

The room dims just a little. I feel like I'm crashing down from cloud nine, my joy colliding with something sharp and familiar. Doubt. Hurt. Anger. Their argument on my birthday comes back with alarming clarity.

I shake it off. I won't let it spoil the night. Not this moment.

"You were right to ask anyway," I say, managing a smile. I lace my fingers through his.

Still smiling, I take a bite of pizza—hot and cheesy, *grounding*. But already, part of me is thinking about the phone call I'll be having later. The things I'll need to say. The things he'll need to hear. But not tonight, tonight is for us.

We take the night and all of Saturday and bask in the feeling—like cats stretching out in the sun. I want to elongate the joy until it touches every corner of us, until it lingers in the air like humidity sticking to every surface

He ends up staying over. We'll see the family tomorrow for Easter. So today is for us.

I wake early to sit with the sunrise again. Lately, it feels like I need to tell it about every beautiful thing that still happens in the world—just in case it's listening.

I hold up my hand, watching my ring catch the orange and gold of the morning light. It still all feels surreal.

I hear the creak of the door and turn. Frank is slipping out.

"What are you doing up so early?"

"Sometimes I like to watch the sunrise," I shrug, nonchalantly. "Is that so strange?"

"When you could be lying in bed, getting more beauty sleep? Then yes."

"Are you saying I need more beauty sleep?"

"Of course not. Leave some beauty for the rest of us, that's what I say. You're *too* beautiful as it is. No more sleep for you, in fact."

I laugh—soft and real—and tug him gently into a kiss.

"Sit with me?" I ask. "It's worth it. I promise."

"Not without coffee first," he grumbles, but he's already moving.

A few minutes later, he returns with two steaming mugs. He hands me one and settles beside me, tucking a second blanket over my lap.

The silence between us is the best kind—easy, full.

"Beautiful, isn't it?" I whisper, watching the sun rise slow and sure over the rooftops.

He looks at me.

"Sorry, my love," he says, voice quiet, eyes warm. "I've got something even more beautiful to compare it to."

Now that it's Easter Sunday, Frank and I are heading to Mike and Annette's after church. My ring feels like it has a spotlight on it. I keep catching sight of it, and every time I do, a flutter of joy rises—only to be weighed down again by the knowledge that my father said no. I still don't know how I'm going to talk to him about it. But today isn't about that.

Today, I get to tell Mike and Annette.

They've been quietly rooting for me and Frank all along. Annette even made Frank homemade chicken soup during his radiation, "to strengthen him back up," she'd said, waving away his protests with a ladle.

Who knows if it helped, but it made him smile, and I love her for that.

We walk through their familiar front door, the smell of lemon and garlic wafting in from the kitchen, and find them exactly where I hoped—seated side by side at the table.

"Guess what," I say, breathless.

I don't wait for an answer.

I just hold up my left hand.

Annette stands so quickly her chair scrapes back against the tile. She covers her mouth with both hands, her eyes already filling.

Mike rises more slowly, but his smile is wide. He reaches out and shakes Frank's hand—firm and steady.

"Welcome to the family," he says.

And just like that, the tears come.

The kids are all dressed in their Easter best, darting around the backyard like they're on personal missions, each one determined to find the most eggs.

The back door creaks open behind me, and my stomach drops before I even turn.

It's Mom and Dad.

Not now.

I don't have the mindshare for this, not today.

They walk toward me, both smiling. Of course. The last time we saw each other was my birthday. Reconciliation. Laughter. But now that feels tainted.

I can feel the anger rising—quiet at first, then faster, sharper, louder. Dad seems to notice and his eyes fall to my hand. His smile fades. His brows furrow.

Then I see it. Clear as day.

Anger.

"Gertrude. No."

I walk toward them, fast.

"You will not tell me no. Not about this."

"I can and I will. *No.*"

"How can you think you have control over this? You must be out of your ever-loving mind."

His eyes flash. "You will not speak to me that way. I'm your father. You will show me some respect."

"I would—if you deserved it!"

I can hear my voice rising. I don't care. "Frank came to you—the man I *love*—and asked for my hand. And you said no? After all this time? After everything you've said about wanting me to get married?"

"Yes," he says, firm. "I do want you to be married. But not to him."

It knocks the breath out of me.

"Excuse me?" I can barely say the words.

"Why not him? Because he's not made of money? Frank has a good job. A steady job. He's kind. He's loyal."

Dad shakes his head, his voice full of urgency—panic, even.

"Because you're setting yourself up for a life of pain, Trudy. Don't you see that? He's not going to be—" He stops himself. "Be with Henry. Henry will take care of you. You'll be happy. You'll have children. You'll have comfort."

"I don't want Henry," I say, and my voice is shaking, but steady. "I never did."

Dad's eyes narrow.

"You're being stupid."

"Don't be this way," I snap. "I chose him. That's that."

"I won't have it!" Dad booms.

"Then *you* marry Henry," I fire back. "Because I'm marrying Frank."

Silence. Thick and immediate.

He stares at me like he doesn't recognize me anymore.

And I feel it then, that fraying line that's been holding us together.

I feel it snap. Quietly. Finally. Like a thread giving out under too much strain. And I don't know if we'll ever get it back.

He digs his heels in. And I dig in mine.

We stand there, my mother between us, while something irrevocably shifts in the air around us.

The children keep playing. Oblivious. Free.

"Please, Trudy. Don't do this," he pleads. "Your life will never be the same."

I meet his eyes. "Isn't that the whole point?"

He looks past me then, like he's searching for something in the distance. Something he can't quite hold onto.

"I can't support this, Trudy. I can't. I can't watch you break your own heart. You're full of life, of color—I don't want that stolen from you."

"You already did that, Dad."

The words land hard. He flinches, like I've slapped him. *Good.*

I turn. Walk away. Toward Frank. Toward my future.

Chapter 11

"A good friend is like a four-leaf clover; hard to find and lucky to have." —
Irish Proverb

After the disaster on Easter, I decide to call Patty and Caroline. I want to tell them about the engagement in person—and we haven't had one of our book gatherings in far too long.

Whenever I tell Mike we're meeting, he always groans and then asks to come.

"Get your own book group," I shoot back.

"Maybe I will, and you won't be invited."

He usually sticks out his tongue in response, which somehow only proves my point.

I suggest *The Crucible* for our next book, and both girls agree without hesitation. Patty's already read it but says she'll give it another glance so we can really dig into it. Caroline promises to grab a copy on her way home from work tomorrow.

When they arrive, they come in like the burst of life they always are. I realize instantly—this is exactly what I needed.

These girls. These nights. These conversations over wine and literature and life.

Patty, ever punctual, is the first to arrive. I sweep her into a hug before she's even through the door.

"Well, hello to you too," she laughs. The bottle of riesling in her hand is cold against my cheek as we hug.

I step back and extend my hand dramatically, the ring catching the light.

She gasps, grabs my hand like she's a diamond appraiser. "Oh my God! You can't be serious!"

"Tell me everything."

"We'll wait for Caroline," I say, grinning.

Caroline arrives not long after, balancing a box of cannoli and a wide smile. I pull her in for a hug next, and go through the same dramatic unveiling of the ring.

Once we're settled—wine poured, pastries on plates—I tell them everything. The pizzeria. The proposal. The blowup on Easter. I feel it all again as I speak, but it's softened now by the comfort of this room, these women, this night.

We settle ourselves in for a long night of laughter and discussions.

I make tea and set out a cheese plate like I'm hosting foreign dignitaries instead of two of my best friends. My engagement ring catches the kitchen light every time I reach for a napkin or pour a cup, and I catch Patty glancing at it more than once with a grin.

We're gathered around my small kitchen table, the worn paperback copy of *The Crucible* between us. The pages are dog-eared and annotated, passed around like gossip. Caroline reads aloud a passage and leans back with a sigh.

"You know what this really is?" she says. "It's men turning on women the minute they stop behaving the way they want them to."

Patty nods, swirling her wine. "Exactly. And they say it's about God and order, but it's just fear. Fear of women who speak their minds. Fear of women who want more. They weren't burning witches. They were burning women they were afraid of."

I rest my chin in my hand and smile at them. "It's just the same today, isn't it? Only now, it's in *whispers* instead of courtrooms. People don't come right out and call you a witch anymore—they just call you difficult. Or selfish. Or too loud. Or not the marrying kind."

"Or that your opinion makes you bossy, or that you're too sensitive if you don't like being called sweetheart or honey by the old fart at work." Says Caroline

Patty leans in. "And yet here you are. Engaged."

"Yes," I say, softly. "To someone they never expected me to choose. Someone they told me not to choose."

There's a beat of quiet, the kind that fills a room with something more than silence. And then Patty lifts her glass.

"To choosing what's right, even when it's hard."

We clink glasses. Outside, the streetlamp flickers on. In here, we are full of light.

Over the next few months, my mother keeps calling, trying to smooth things over.

"He was in shock."

"He'll come around."

"He's just so worried about you."

I've heard it all.

But I still won't speak to him. It was too much—too cruel. And my mother's defense of him only makes it worse. Eventually, I tell her I don't want Dad at the wedding.

"If he can't support this, I don't want him there."

"My love, it's not that he doesn't support you—"

From the other room, my father shouts, "I cannot support my daughter throwing away her future! How do you expect me to?"

I sigh into the phone. "You were saying, Mom? Look— I'm not going to debate this. I'm happy. That's that."

Then, like clockwork, he asks to get on the phone, but every time my father gets on the line, he's met with the dial tone. This is not the first time we've had this conversation. I doubt it will be the last.

Frank and I quickly realize we'll be paying for the wedding ourselves—which is fine by us. He's been estranged from his family for years, so he's just happy to have a family in me. And in Mike and Annette.

The kids are falling more in love with him every day. He's always making up games, pulling out crayons and glue for some wild art project, or making them laugh with a joke so bad it's good.

He's over almost every day now. Before he leaves, he always tucks a little note somewhere for me to find—something sweet, funny, or just a "thinking of you"—so I have something to read on my way to work or to stumble across while I'm cleaning. So, I start leaving him notes, too—slipping them into his coat pockets or between the pages of whatever book he's reading. It's become a bit of a game. Half the fun is trying to sneak them in without him noticing. He's caught me a few times, which usually ends with him wrestling the note out of my hands, then covering my face in kisses until I'm laughing too hard to protest. So really, I'm not complaining.

I'm digging through the drawer for one of Frank's notes when I spot a letter mixed in with the rest of the mail. My heart sinks. It's from Henry.

Just the sight of his handwriting sends a cold sweat creeping up my back. Our last encounter... wasn't pleasant.

I stare at the envelope for a few minutes, as if waiting will somehow soften what's inside. Like time could build a shield between me and his words.

But it doesn't. And I know I have to read it. I take a deep breath and tear open the envelope.

Dear Trudy,

You really did it.

I heard from mutual friends—of course I did. You're engaged. To that other guy. And all I can think is: how could you?

We had something real. Something smart. Something that made sense.

You knew the life we could have had. You saw it. I painted it for you in full color—a home, family, security, respect. And you nodded along, like you understood. Like you wanted it. And now you've gone and thrown it all away.

For what? A gamble? A feeling? Some spark that'll burn out the second real life shows up with bills and decisions and broken things that need fixing?

You think this is love, but it's a fantasy. You don't even realize what you're walking away from. You could've had everything. With me, you would've been taken care of. You would've had a name people respected. A future you didn't have to worry about. But instead, you've chosen... what? Struggle? A man who will never offer you the life I could? Who won't be around forever?

I don't know when you stopped thinking clearly. Maybe you never were. Maybe I gave you too much credit. I thought you were smart, Trudy. I really did. But now? Now I just see someone playing house with a ticking clock and calling it romance.

Here's the truth: women like you don't get many chances. And you just wasted yours.

When it all falls apart—and it will—don't expect me to be there. You made your choice. Don't come running when you realize what you gave up.

—Henry

I let out a long breath. I understand that he's angry, but every part of me feels so calm with the understanding that I have chosen the right man for me. I crumple up the letter and throw it in the garbage, not feeling the slightest urge to reply. This life we're building—it's good. It's happy. And I'm leaning into it with everything I've got.

Chapter 12

May 6, 1964

My Trudy,

I woke up this morning and found one of your hairs on my shirt—how it got there, I don't know, but I didn't want to brush it off. Isn't that strange? A single hair. It made me feel like you were still here, like maybe your laughter would come floating in from the kitchen any second. Maybe I'm getting sentimental in my old age. Twenty-nine is practically antique, after all.

I don't say it enough (or maybe I say it too often, but never quite right), but I love you. Not just in the big, dramatic way people throw around in the movies—but in the quiet ways. Like the way you scrunch your nose when you're thinking. Or how you sing under your breath when you're folding laundry. Or how you write things in the margins of books like they're secrets you're sharing only with yourself.

I think if I could live inside one of your margins, I'd be a lucky man.

Planning this wedding with you, even the tiny parts, makes me feel like I've already won something. Even if it's just deciding what cake we should have or which family member we'll politely uninvite. Some days I still feel the ache in my bones from the radiation, but I don't tell you that part much. Not because I want to hide it, but because you already carry so much. You've chosen me—just as I am, uncertainty and all. That kind of love feels like a miracle. You make this life beautiful, even on the hardest days.

I'll bring dinner tonight—don't cook. Unless, of course, you're planning to make that lemon chicken again, in which case I take it all back.

Always yours,

Frank

May 30, 1964

My dearest Frank,

The sun hit my hand this morning while I was pouring tea, and for a second I forgot. The light caught the ring and bounced off the wall, and I just stared at it like I'd never seen it before. I must have looked ridiculous, standing there holding the kettle mid-air, completely frozen. But I couldn't help it——my breath caught. You chose it. You chose me. I still don't fully believe it's real.

Sometimes I catch myself doing completely normal things——folding laundry, grading papers, peeling an orange——and then I feel the ring shift slightly on my finger and my heart stumbles. I'm yours. You're mine. That's the realest thing I know right now.

I wish I could say everything was perfect. I'm still so angry with my father... He didn't even ask to see the ring. I just cannot believe he didn't give you his blessing! Well, we don't need it! Or him! I wish I could shake him——make him see you the way I do.

Mom has been quiet, but I think she's working on him. You know how she is——soft voice, slow steps, but hopefully she'll help him see reason. I'm hoping she'll help him see this isn't a phase, or rebellion, or whatever else he's trying to turn it into. I'm not chasing a fantasy.

I'm choosing the kindest, strongest, most grounded man I've ever known.

I hope you're resting tonight. You tend to carry other people's worries on your shoulders without even realizing it, and I want you to let them down for a bit. Just for tonight. I'll carry them for both of us if I have to.

I love you. I love you so much it scares me sometimes.

Yours always,

Trudy

June 2, 1964

Trudy, my love,

I know you're angry. Believe me, I understand—and I'd never tell you where to put your feelings (though if you decide to throw something, aim away from my typewriter). What I will ask is that you give your father a little grace. I see in his eyes how deeply he loves you; it pours out of him. And who could blame him? I'm angry too. But you don't need anyone's permission to marry who you love, and for that I am so grateful. Grateful, too, that you always listen to that beautiful mind of yours (even if it occasionally forgets where it left the house keys).

This life we're going to build will be so full of love we won't know what to do with it all. Maybe we'll bottle the extra and sell it—finally a family business your father could approve of.

Be mad, or don't. Forgive him, or don't. I'm in your corner. Always.

All my love,

Frank

June 24, 1964

(the day before I say goodbye to chalky fingers, loud lunchrooms, and little shoelaces that never stay tied——for a whole two months!)

My dear Frank,

I'm writing this from my desk, during what might be the longest free period in recorded history. The classroom is half-packed, my bulletin board looks naked, and I found a single shoe under my desk this morning. No one's claimed it. I've decided to name it Herbert.

Tomorrow's the last day of school, and I feel like a balloon that's slowly deflating——not in a sad way, just that I've given everything I had to give this year. I can feel it in my feet, my spine, and the smudge of chalk on my elbow that I've stopped trying to wash off. But I've also never felt more certain that I chose the right path. Even on the hard days. Even when I'm counting down to summer like the kids are.

The only thing that makes this week sweeter is knowing what I get to come home to. Our dinners together.

Frank, you've become the rhythm of my days in ways I never expected. You leave me notes in the morning like you're still wooing me——which, if I'm being honest, is entirely unfair because I'm already head over heels. It's like chasing someone who's already yours. But please don't stop.

I've been thinking about that night at the pizza place——the ring box, the way your hands trembled just a little. The way mine did too. The way the world seemed to tilt into something new and entirely ours.

I know things are still a little messy with my father. And I know you worry sometimes that you're dragging weight behind you. But if you are, let me carry some of it. We're building something that feels stronger than fear and softer than certainty. And it's beautiful. Not perfect, not always easy——but so beautiful.

Tomorrow, after I wave goodbye to my last student and take down the last crooked poster, I'm coming straight to you. And maybe we can go somewhere——with good food, bad napkins, and no agenda. Or maybe we'll just sit outside with your sketchpad and my lemonade and let summer begin.

Love you madly,

Trudy

P.S. I think Herbert wants to meet you. You two have the same quiet mystery about you.

August 20, 1964

My darling Trudy,

I keep thinking about Bear Mountain. About the way you laughed when your hair got caught in that low-hanging branch. The way you pointed out flowers like you were introducing me to old friends. The way we floated across Hessian Lake in that kayak, drifting like we had all the time in the world. We didn't talk much then—we didn't have to. I've never known peace the way I do when I'm beside you.

I pressed one of the wildflowers you picked in the pages of my book. It's still there. Still bright, still whole. Just like you, like us. I think I'll carry that afternoon with me always— your sun-warmed shoulder brushing mine, the picnic blanket soft beneath us, the world pausing long enough for us to just be. There's a stillness in me now, a kind I never had before you. I think it's what people mean when they say home.

Yours,

Frank

September 29, 1964

Dear Frank,

I meant to write this earlier in the weekend, but I blinked and somehow it's already Sunday night again. How does that keep happening?

School has officially been back in session for a few weeks now, and I have to admit——year two feels a little less like being thrown into the deep end without knowing how to swim. I'm not exactly doing laps, but at least I'm treading water without gasping. Most days, anyway.

Mrs. DeMarco has been a godsend, as always. She still checks in every afternoon like clockwork, pokes her head in with her thermos of coffee and that same line: "You surviving, Kirchberger?" I tell her I am, and we both pretend not to notice when I let out a sigh of relief loud enough to rattle the coat hooks.

There are, of course, still hiccups. One little boy tried to flush an entire package of crayons down the toilet on Wednesday——he said he wanted to see if the pipes "made rainbows." (They did not.) And someone keeps leaving notes in the library books that say things like "Sister Mary has x-ray vision." I haven't caught the culprit yet, but I think I'm hot on their trail. There was some frosting left on one of the notes, which feels like a solid lead in the case.

But in between all that, something is clicking. I feel more sure of myself——more steady, I guess. Like I belong in front of that classroom now, instead of borrowing someone else's job. I think about last fall and how nervous I was, how everything felt so new and uncertain. And now… it's still uncertain, but it doesn't feel new anymore. It feels mine.

Anyway, I just wanted to tell you all that, and to say that I miss you. I keep imagining what you'd say if you saw the state of my teacher's desk——it looks like a bomb went off in a paper factory. You'd probably raise that one eyebrow and make some joke about needing a permit just to walk near it. (You'd be right.)

I hope work hasn't swallowed you whole and that you're taking some time to breathe. Write when you can——even a few lines. I keep your last note tucked into the front cover of my lesson planner like a lucky charm.

Always yours,

Trudy

October 3, 1964

Dear Trudy,

First of all, if your student really did manage to get rainbows out of the plumbing, I'd have nominated him for a Nobel Prize on the spot. Please advise if I should alert the science committee—or at least add it to the next article for The Daily News.

Second, I'm relieved to hear year two has you treading water rather than drowning. Although, knowing you, I doubt you're anywhere near drowning. More likely, you're already doing water ballet and just refusing to give yourself credit for how remarkable you are.

As for your desk, I have no doubt it's every bit the disaster you describe. I'll come inspect it myself one of these days and issue the proper citations. (Don't worry, I'll waive the fine in exchange for a sandwich and one of those apple strudels your mother smuggles my way.)

Work has, in fact, tried to swallow me whole, but I fought back with coffee and sarcasm. I miss you too—more than I'll ever be able to put on paper. Keep your lucky charm close; I'll keep writing, if only to keep the x-ray sisters from catching my spelling mistakes.

Yours (with both eyebrows raised),
Frank

October 27, 1964

My dearest Frank,

I stopped by the corner store after school today and——you guessed it——I bought us cat ears. Two pairs. Matching. I hope you're ready to embrace your feline side, because this year, we're going as cats. Together. Caroline's party is on Saturday, and I expect full participation, whiskers and all.

(And don't you dare just wear your regular clothes and claim to be a "cool cat." I know all your tricks.)

The kids at school are completely off their rockers this week. It's like Halloween cast a spell and turned them all into little goblins with a sugar radar. I confiscated three packs of candy corn, one whoopee cushion, and a Dracula cape——today.

I've been thinking about last Halloween a lot lately. Remember, sheriff? That noisy little party, everyone laughing and yelling, and somehow we found the quietest spot on that lumpy old couch and just... talked. For hours. The noise faded and it was just us. You with your quiet smile and me pretending not to be completely swept away.

And here we are, a year later, still talking, still laughing, still finding the quiet together——even in the middle of chaos.

I can't wait to show up to that party with you this year. Love you always,

Your Cat

P.S. I dare you to meow at me in front of Caroline. Double dare.

December 22, 1964

My Trudy,

I can't stop thinking about Christmas Eve.

It's been running through my head all week—the stories you've told me, the tree run, the secret delivery mission, the way everything transforms just in time for the kids to come bursting back through the door. It sounds like something out of a movie. And this year, I get to be part of it. Not just a bystander, not just your date... but your fiancé. I still can't say that word without grinning like an idiot.

You know, I never really had anything like that growing up. Our holidays were quieter, simpler. A tree, some lights, a big meal. But this—your family's Christmas Eve—is something else entirely. It's joyful and chaotic and full of purpose, like everyone's been assigned a role in a secret holiday play. I love that the magic doesn't just happen... you all make it happen.

And I get to help.

Tell your dad I'm ready for tree duty. Tell Mike I'll help keep an eye out for Santa (though between us, I'm just hoping to catch a glimpse of his sleigh reflected in your eyes). Tell Annette I'll carry as many presents as she needs me to—no complaints. And most of all, tell the kids I'll be watching the skies with them next year too, if they'll have me.

I can already picture it: the ornaments on the coffee table, the eggnog in coffee cups, the Linzer tarts, the moment when the front door opens and everyone freezes mid-motion like they've been caught by magic itself. I'll probably be holding a strand of tinsel, trying not to laugh. Trying not to cry.

This is the kind of moment you remember for the rest of your life. And I get to be standing right beside you in it.

Thank you for bringing me into your world.

Yours always,

Frank

December 27, 1964

My darling Frank,

I keep playing it over in my head——Christmas Eve, the lights, the laughter, the way you fit so seamlessly into everything like you'd always been there. And I just keep thinking: this is it. This is the life I want.

You were wonderful. Not just helpful (though you were, of course—— tree-lifter, ornament-hanger, gift-carrier extraordinaire), but present in that way you always are. You saw everyone. You made the kids laugh. You made Mom smile when she didn't think anyone was looking. You even got a nod of approval from Dad, which, as you know, right now is equivalent to a full standing ovation.

When the front door opened and the kids ran in to find the tree lit and the living room transformed, I watched their faces——but I also watched yours. You had that same look of quiet awe. That same joy. Like you knew this was something sacred and silly all at once. And when you reached for my hand, it was all I needed.

Having you there made everything feel different——in the best way. Not like I was sharing a tradition, but like we were starting something new, together. A beginning tucked inside an old, familiar rhythm.

I hope you felt it too—the magic, the belonging, the love. You are part of all of it now, and I can't tell you how happy that makes me. Truly happy, deep-down-in-my-bones kind of happy.

I love you. I loved watching you become part of our Christmas, and become rooted into our family. I can't wait for every Christmas to come.

Yours forever,

Trudy

December 30, 1964

Dear Trudy,

Thank you for the wonderful Christmas gift, though I should probably be thanking myself, considering how hard I had to work to keep you from peeking at yours under the tree. Watching you "casually" circle the presents like a detective staking out a crime scene may have been the real gift this year.

You'll be glad to know the wrapping paper survived your not-so-subtle inspections.

I love it... almost as much as I love you, but actually not even close.

Next year, I'm putting your presents in a safe deposit box just to see what lengths you'll go to.

Merry Christmas, Trudy.
Always,
Frank

January 1, 1965

My dearest Frank,

Happy New Year, my love.

I'm writing this with a slight headache, a lipstick-smudged champagne glass still sitting by the sink, and bits of confetti clinging to the hem of my skirt. I want to get it all down before it fades——because ringing in the New Year at Caroline's apartment last night (and by rang, I mean shouted, danced, clinked, and hollered it in with what must've been half of Woodside crammed into four tiny rooms) was perfect.

It was loud. And silly. And so much fun. Caroline's "fancy" hors d'oeuvres——Ritz crackers with an assortment of mysterious toppings——were a hit, and I'm still not sure we ever figured out who brought those noisemakers that sounded like a duck trapped in a wind tunnel. I laughed until my stomach hurt.

Right before midnight, someone turned off the lights——still no idea who——but I want to kick them, because that's why I ended up kissing your cheek instead of your lips. I couldn't find your face fast enough in the chaos.

And through it all, I kept thinking about last year——how you missed the countdown entirely. You'd dozed off on the couch and barely made it to the pub in time, but we still had our kiss.

I don't know what this year will bring, but if it has even half the love we've already found, then I know we'll be okay. Better than okay.

Here's to 1965. To laughter and soft blankets. To noise and quiet. To us.

All my love,

Trudy

P.S. Caroline says you're a good dancer and she wants you on her team next time we play charades. So, you've been warned.

January 2, 1965

My Trudy,

I've finally shaken the last of the tinsel out of my shoes, which I'm convinced was a deliberate ploy on your part to keep Christmas with me a little longer. (If so—well played.)

I've been thinking about our tree. Your apartment may be small, but that tree? That tree had personality. A little crooked, slightly overzealous in the lights department, and entirely ours. I loved every inch of it.

And the ornament.

I stared at it again this morning—the one you gave me: a small silver circle with "Engaged 1964" etched on it. I never imagined I'd have something like that hanging on a tree. And yet there it was, catching the light like it belonged there all along.

Like I belonged there.

It's tucked away now in tissue paper like something sacred, and I'm already looking forward to the moment next December when we unwrap it again. Maybe we'll hang it on a slightly bigger tree. Maybe we'll be in a place with a little more space. But I know I'll still be thinking the same thing: How lucky I am to have found you.

And as for that New Year's Eve party—I don't think my hearing has fully recovered. Caroline's apartment has the acoustics of a cannonball and the size of a shoebox, but somehow it fit more laughter than any ballroom I've ever been in. I can't remember the last time I laughed that hard while holding a paper cup of warm champagne.

Now, regarding Caroline's note about my "dance moves"—I'd like it formally entered into the record that any and all rhythm I exhibited that night was a direct result of watching you. The way you moved in that crowded living room, your arms full of sparkler light and mischief—well, let's just say you made it easy to follow your lead.

Charades team or not, she'll have to fight you for me on the next slow song.

I loved spending this holiday season with you. Waking up beside you. Watching you hum along to carols while making French toast in your pajamas—your hair still wild from sleep. It felt like stepping into the life I didn't know I'd been waiting for. One with cluttered stockings, burnt toast, and the way your eyes light up when you hand me a gift you've clearly been dying to give for weeks.

You're the best thing about this holiday, Trudy. You're the best thing about any day.

Yours, always,

Frank

P.S. I'm still claiming victory in the gingerbread decorating contest. The judges (me) were unanimous.

P. P.S. I noticed you didn't keep score, but someone ate my gingerbread man's arm and replaced it with a candy cane. I have my suspicions. (It made him look like a festive pirate, so I let it slide.)

January 16, 1965

My Future Husband Frank,

I have a little list of venues I want us to look at together, and just writing that makes my heart race. Can you believe we're actually at this stage? It's starting to feel <u>so</u> <u>real</u>... the kind of real that comes with centerpieces, vows, and very expensive price tags. (Don't worry, I promise I'll only fall in love with the ones that don't require us to sell a kidney.)

I can't wait to see them with you and to remind myself that the only part I really care about is you.

Always yours,
Trudy

P.S. I'm going to have to call Annette to go dress shopping with me soon. Do you think I should invite Mom, Patty and Caroline too? They'll have lots of opinions, I'm sure; though between the four of them, I may need a referee more than a seamstress. I should probably bring a whistle just in case.

February 15, 1965

My Trudy,

Well, we did it.

The venue is booked, the church is ours, and I still can't believe I get to marry you—not just in theory, but in a real place, with pews and everything. I think I smiled the whole drive home (which is impressive, considering I got lost twice getting back from the church and had to stop for directions at a gas station where the attendant called me "sir lovebird").

I keep picturing you walking down the aisle, and it hits me like a brand new thought each time—she's going to be my wife. That word feels so big and wonderful and surreal when it's you.

Valentine's Day was perfect. The little heart you drew on my napkin at lunch is now in my wallet, right behind your photo. Might have to frame it next to the engagement ornament. (I told you I'm sentimental.)

We're really doing it, Trudy. You and me. The church on Long Island is beautiful, but honestly, you could marry me in a broom closet and I'd still be the happiest man alive. (Though I admit, your mom might object.)

All my love,

Frank

March 16, 1965

My darling Frank,

First of all—thank you again for my birthday gift. Our new little kitten is the perfect addition to the life we're creating together. I've decided to name him Smokey, in case I forgot to tell you. I still haven't stopped smiling.

That said—and I say this with love in my heart and a very practical voice in my head—we do need to start watching our spending. I know you'd buy me the moon if you could (and you've probably tried), but October is coming faster than we think. That wedding dress isn't going to pay for itself, and I'd rather not honeymoon in the backyard. (Although, with you, even that would be pretty wonderful.)

Speaking of—where are we going to honeymoon? I keep picturing somewhere quiet and warm, just the two of us, maybe a little beach and a lot of naps. But I want to know what you think. If you say "upstate," I swear I'll hide your socks. (Kidding. Mostly.)

Don't forget to write me back. Or better yet—tell me over dinner, because I miss you already and it's only been a few hours.

Forever yours (and budgeting responsibly),

Trudy

P.S. I've circled the calendar date for October 23rd three times now. Just saying.

P.P.S. Tell your socks I was joking.

March 18, 1965

Dear Trudy,

Consider this my official promise to be very aware of spending from now on—but when I saw that little gray ball of mischief, all my good intentions went right out the window. Smokey had you written all over him. I couldn't help myself.

Knowing you'll both be waiting for me and that after we're married, we'll all live together, the three of us—filled me with more love than I knew what to do with. For once, my head lost the argument to my heart, and I think I made the right choice.

Yours (and Smokey's),
Frank

P.S. Remind Smokey that my side of the bed is still mine. I'd rather not have to arm wrestle a kitten for pillow space.

April 26, 1965

My darling Frank,

Thank you—truly—for the most wonderful weekend. I still feel like I'm floating a little, like there's music under my feet and spring in my bones.

Fiddler on the Roof was everything I hoped it would be and more. I laughed, I cried, I hummed "If I Were a Rich Man" under my breath all the way back to the hotel. (You, by the way, do a very convincing Tevye—though I think the man next to us was startled when you started clapping along with the bottle dance.) I keep thinking about that final scene—how quiet the theater got, how I reached for your hand without even realizing it. And how you were already holding mine.

And the hotel—what a treat. The two of us tucked away above the city, the soft sheets, the room-service coffee (which somehow tasted better just because it arrived on a tray), and waking up next to you with the city just starting to stir outside the window. I don't think I'll ever get over the feeling of starting a morning with you. You make even ordinary things feel touched by magic.

The MoMA was dreamy. I don't know if it was the art or the way you whispered commentary like a rogue tour guide, but I haven't laughed that much in a museum in ages. That painting with the red dot? I'm still not convinced you didn't make up half of what you said about it——but I believed you in the moment, which is a testament to either your charm or my gullibility.

And then the park in the afternoon sun, trees just starting to bloom, everyone around us acting like the city had been waiting all winter to exhale. That ice cream vendor gave us way too much——though I suspect your grin had something to do with that.

It was a lovely day. A perfect day. The kind that feels like a postcard I want to keep forever.

I'm back at my desk now, papers to grade and laundry to fold, but I keep drifting back to you. To us. To the rhythm of walking beside you, talking about nothing and everything, and feeling so sure——so certain——that I am exactly where I'm meant to be.

All my love,

Trudy

P.S. I found the theater ticket stub in my coat pocket. I'm tucking it into my journal. You know——just in case we get old and sentimental. (As if we aren't already.)

P.P.S. While this weekend was absolutely lovely — but if we don't start buckling down soon, our guests will have to bring their own cake. (Maybe we can call it a "potluck wedding" and pretend it was intentional?)

May 9, 1965

Trudy, my love—

I meant to say this in person but you were halfway out the door with coffee in one hand and your school bag in the other (you are the most beautiful whirlwind I've ever seen):

You need to tell Annette.

About being your maid of honor, I mean. Before she hears it from Mike and I get kicked out of the family.

Because yes—I asked Mike to be my best man. He said yes, gave me a bear hug that nearly cracked a rib, and immediately started brainstorming tux colors. (Apparently "eggplant" is on the table. I told him you'd veto that faster than Theresa can do a cartwheel.)

Anyway, Annette deserves the official ask from you.

Also—just so you know—your "wedding binder" is now occupying approximately 40% of my nightstand. And I wouldn't have it any other way.

Love you more every day,

Frank

P.S. I saw the note you slipped in my lunch bag. It made me laugh like an idiot in the break room. You're the best part of my day.

May 15, 1965

My Darling Frank,

I loved having you with me at Mike's birthday... it just felt right. He hasn't stopped talking about that book you gave him, and I could tell how much it meant to him. You're so thoughtful, and seeing you with him, with all of us, made me so happy. Watching you slip right into the kids' games "pretending" to let Michael Jr. beat you at chess (we all know he won fair and square), playing peek-a-boo with Denise until she was belly-laughing, painting right alongside Theresa, and dancing around the table with Karen... it made it all feel even more like you're already part of the family. It feels like we're not just celebrating birthdays anymore, but slowly building our own little family together. And I wouldn't want to do that with anyone else.

Always yours,
Trudy

P.S. Don't worry, I'm going to ask Annette to be my maid of honor this week... unless you think Mike would look better in a sash and holding my bouquet.

June 25, 1965

My Trudy,

School's out! I can practically hear the collective sigh of relief from teachers all over New York, but mostly I'm just thrilled you're done. No more early morning rushes, no more stacks of spelling quizzes, no more cafeteria mystery meat. Just summer—and you.

I'm so proud of you, you know. Another year in the books. I know it wasn't always easy, but you made it through, and the kids are lucky to have you. Now it's your turn to rest, to laugh, to wake up slow, and to wear sandals far more than anyone in a professional setting would ever allow.

To kick it off properly, I say we celebrate—just you and me. How do you feel about Coney Island this weekend? We could ride the Wonder Wheel, split a paper tray of fries, and I'll try to win you one of those impossibly ugly stuffed animals at the ring toss (you can name it something ironic and give it a place of honor in your apartment). And of course, we can end the night on the Ferris Wheel.

And while we're dreaming of summer plans—what do you say we take a little trip? Nothing fancy, nothing that'll break our wedding budget, but just enough of a getaway to mark this season as ours. I'll follow your lead. A cabin in the Catskills?

A sleepy beach town? A borrowed tent and a few bug bites if we must? Tell me what sounds like us.

I want long days with you. I want ice cream dripping down our wrists and evening walks where we don't notice how far we've gone until we have to double back. I want books read side by side, naps in patches of sun, and one of those quiet little memories we'll look back on years from now and say, "Remember that summer?"

Let me know what you're craving, my love. The map is wide open.

Yours, already dreaming,

Frank

P.S. I'm bringing sunscreen this time. You're not getting pink on my watch—not on my beach day.

July 5, 1965

Dear Frank,

I'm sitting on the porch with a cold lemonade and sunburned knees, thinking about yesterday. The kids are still asleep, Karen curled up with the seashells we collected like they're treasure. I guess to her, they are.

That was one of the best Fourths I can remember. Not because it was perfect—because it wasn't. I avoided Dad like it was a party game and lost spectacularly at charades (Theresa's "Statue of Liberty" impression was hard to beat). But it was still so good. So full.

Watching you with the kids, handing out sparklers like they were gold coins... flipping burgers while Michael Jr. gave you "grill advice"... running through the sand with Denise on your shoulders—it felt like something steady and real. Something that could last.

I noticed you joking around with Dad. You always know how to disarm people, even him. I don't know what you said, but he laughed. Thank you for trying, even when it's hard. Even when he doesn't deserve it.

The bungalow was magic. That soft late-day light, the smell of saltwater, you holding my hand while the waves touched our toes—it all felt like the life we're building is already here in pieces. Scattered like shells on the beach, just waiting for us to pick them up.

I love you, Frank. Days like yesterday just make it all feel even clearer.

Love always,

Trudy

P.S. I found the tiniest shell in my pocket this morning. I'm keeping it in my wallet—just a little reminder.

September 7, 1965

My Trudy,

First things first—good luck today, teacher. I know those kids don't stand a chance with you at the front of the room. They'll be spelling better, sitting straighter, and smiling brighter by the end of the week. I only wish I could be a fly on the wall for that first "Good morning, class." I bet even the chalk listens when you speak.

Now—onto something else. I found a place.

We can add flowers outside. Nothing fancy, but the windows are big and there's room for my easel and things I've saved from Korea. It's only about a 10-minute walk from your place, so it won't be far. (Not that I have been, lately—I'm fairly certain your neighbors already assume I live with you.) The landlord says I can move in next week. I figured I should tell you before you find my socks folded in your kitchen drawer again.

I know we're making a life slowly, piece by piece. This feels like the next right one. Close to your old place, but still our own. And hey, once we're married, we'll have to figure out who gets which side of the bed officially.

But for now, I'll be waiting after school with a cup of tea and a few jokes I'm workshopping. Bad ones, I promise. Don't let the nuns steal your sparkle today. You're going to shine.

All my love (and then some),

Frank

P.S. I left a note in your lunch bag too. Try not to read it until you're on break—unless you want to cry in the supply closet again.

October 1, 1965

My almost-~~husband~~ Frank,

We made it, Frank! ~~It's our wedding month~~! I don't know how to explain it except to say that my whole body feels like it's vibrating with ~~joy~~. I'm so excited I can hardly sit still, like one of my own students who knows recess is just minutes away. Every time I think of us... of our wedding, of calling you my husband... I feel like I might burst.

Even the world looks different. The leaves have turned to fire, but somehow, they seem brighter, richer, more alive than they've ever been. I see gold in the trees, red at my feet, and I swear the air itself smells sweeter. It feels like the whole season is celebrating right along with us.

There is a small sadness in me too, that my father can't feel this joy with me. I wish he could. But I am so grateful that we're not walking through this alone. We have my mother, Mike and Annette, and Caroline and Patty cheering us on at every turn. Their support wraps around me like a quilt, warm and reassuring. Or like a cup of tea, warming me from the inside out.

But more than anything, I have you. And that is what steadies me when the days get overwhelming——knowing that very soon, we begin the rest of our lives together. I can hardly wait.

Always yours (and always giddy),

Trudy

P.S. This countdown feels harder to wait for than summer vacation and Christmas morning combined, and you know how _impatient_ I am for both.

Chapter 13

"We loved with a love that was more than love." — Edgar Allan Poe

Living life with Frank has been a dream. He's everything I could want in a man. We've been looking for an apartment, and it seems like he's found one—not too far away, and big enough for both of us. The idea that we'll finally be living under the same roof does something to my heart I can't quite put into words. It'll be ready for us to move into right after we're married.

We've been saving diligently for our wedding (with the occasional splurge every so often). It'll be a modest affair, but one full of love, laughter, and life—the kind of day that feels just like us. The wedding party will be small: just Mike and Annette. I told my dad again that if he can't support my choice, then he shouldn't bother showing up. My mom, of course, is more than welcome. Frank's family isn't going to come, and he seems unbothered by it. My father still refuses to accept that this is my future. I've given him time, space, every chance—but he won't bend. That man is so stubborn.

It's finally the morning of our wedding. I've been looking forward to this day for so long, it felt like it would never come. I feel anxious and excited—like life is about to start for real, with him. We've decided to honeymoon in

264

Bermuda, and I can almost feel the sand between my toes already. October feels like the right time for us, somehow. I keep thinking back to that first Halloween together, sitting on a crowded couch at a party, feeling like we were the only two people in the world. It's funny how that feeling never really went away.

I woke up early again. Watching the sunrise has become a quiet comfort for me. I take my blanket and tea out to the balcony and watch the colors stretch through the clouds— like hope trying to break through the clawing weight that sadness sometimes leaves behind.

These mornings help.

I try to let go of my fear—fear that Frank might relapse, or that I'll never speak to my father again. I try not to cling to those quiet moments when I catch Frank checking his neck in the mirror, or when he tires more easily than he used to. I breathe out all of that anxiety into the crisp fall air.

Today is for love. Nothing else.

Three good things. Today should be easy.

1. It's my wedding day
2. My dress is beautiful
3. Today I become Mrs. Trudy Madden

By 9 a.m., I'm at Mike and Annette's to get ready. The church and reception hall are near them, so it makes sense to spend the morning together. I do my makeup while Annette and my mom help with my hair. Their hands make fast, practiced work of creating something beautiful. They add volume and curl the ends under, and when they're done, it feels... timeless. Like me, but the best possible version.

Annette adds a small piece on top to anchor my veil, then my mother swoops in and delicately pins it into place.

I look at myself in the mirror—still in my robe, makeup done, veil cascading over my shoulders—and it feels surreal. Like the moment is somehow both mine and not mine at the same time.

They give me a quiet moment to breathe and step out to get themselves dressed. I take a few long, slow breaths and let the stillness wash over me.

Earlier, my mom kissed my cheek and told me she wanted to get dressed at home—no matter how silly I said it was.

"All my things are there," she said with a wave of her hand, as if that settled it.

"But we're so close to the church here. You could've just gotten ready with us."

"I won't be long," she said, brushing my cheek with her thumb. "And you're going to be beautiful, my Trud-a-la. I'll meet you at the church."

Then Annette walks back in.

I gasp.

"Annette... you look beautiful."

She's wearing the maid of honor dress we picked together—deep blue, sequined on the top, with silk falling from the waist to the floor. She waves a hand dismissively.

"Oh, please."

She smiles and walks over.

"Let's get you in your gown."

She helps me into my dress, and together we turn toward the mirror. I feel the tears building again—rising fast, catching in my throat.

There I am. A bride.

The dress is long-sleeved, with scalloped lace tracing across my chest and dipping into a fitted waist. A delicate satin ribbon wraps around the middle, giving way to a full satin skirt that flares to the floor in soft, sweeping folds. My veil falls just to my elbows, sheer and light, like a whisper over my shoulders.

It's beautiful. I can hardly believe it's me. And I cannot wait to see Frank.

"I didn't know if we'd even get to today," I whisper. "Not after his diagnosis…"

"I know," she says softly. "But you're here. And he'll be waiting for you at the end of that aisle. So don't smear your eyeliner."

The kids come bursting in, full of energy and wide-eyed wonder. They tell me I look beautiful and beg to come with me, even just for a minute. I laugh and hug them, pulling them in close.

Our bouquets are laid out neatly on the bed—Annette's is full of bright orange roses, and mine is white roses and baby's breath, soft and simple.

I pull a few stems from mine and hand them to Karen, who immediately gets to work making flower crowns. Her fingers move quickly, all focus and pride, and before I know it, she's made one for herself and one for Theresa.

They place them on their heads with reverence, like tiny queens, and I can't help but smile.

Once we're at the church, everything moves quickly—until it doesn't. Until it's time to open the doors and begin the procession.

The doors open.

And there he is.

Our eyes lock. In that moment, it's just us. No one else exists. The room, the guests, the whispers—all of it melts away. Then the swell of the organ rises, a gentle cue: it's time to walk.

I take a step. I walk alone toward him, holding my bouquet tightly, every muscle straining with the quiet urge to run. To run to him. To our life.

I finally reach him—a walk that felt like it took a lifetime.

And in a way, it did.

With every step, I walked away from Trudy Kirchberger and toward Trudy Madden. I take his hand and hold on. To him. To us. To our forever.

When we're pronounced husband and wife, something lifts inside me—a weight I didn't fully realize I'd been carrying. My body feels lighter. My heart, unburdened.

I glance out at our guests with a smile so big it can barely fit in my face. Patty and Caroline are sitting together in a pew, each with dates I don't recognize, and it makes me laugh to myself. Their grins are taking up their entire faces.

I spot Petey—and I swear there's a tear on his cheek. The old softy.

Mrs. DeMarco is there too, sitting beside who I assume is her husband, smiling that quiet, knowing smile—the kind people wear when they're watching something romantic and remembering their own love.

And then I see him.

A pair of familiar eyes.

My father's.

He's sitting in the back of the church beside my mother, eyes shining with tears he refuses to let fall, gripping her hand as tightly as I'm holding Frank's. It stirs something in my heart.

The rest of the day is a blur of kisses, speeches and dancing. It's the happiest day of my life. Before I know it, we're being showered in rice, laughing as we climb into the car and drive off to our honeymoon in Bermuda.

Chapter 14

"Love is composed of a single soul inhabiting two bodies."

— Aristotle

We settle into marriage like it was always waiting for us.

The years pass in snapshots—Saturday mornings with the paper and too much coffee with our cat Smokey at our feet, late-night painting sessions where I fall asleep on the couch while he works beside me, Sunday evenings spent in friendly debates—ones that often turn into long, meandering conversations—over which organizations we can afford to support. There are beach days with the kids collecting shells, and quiet dinners, just the two of us. Grading papers while he edits for *The Daily News*. Keeping our promise to travel whenever and wherever we can.

We build a life out of the ordinary, and it feels extraordinary—because it's ours.

There are jokes and bills and holidays, but mostly jokes. There are long drives and silly fights and sleepy apologies. There are sunrises and birthday candles and love notes scattered around the apartment. There is so much love—steady, full, and simple. It's the life people dream of.

We travel like the world belongs to us. Because during this time, it feels like it does. We want to see the world while we had the chance. We know there's a possibility that our time is fleeting, though neither of us will acknowledge it. So we keep going, keep moving. If we can leave pieces of ourselves behind in every corner of the world, then maybe our story will never truly end. We'll tuck into it places no one would think to look. Everywhere we go, we leave our mark—like pressing our thumbprint into the fabric of the world itself. Then we collect postcards, not just as souvenirs, but as reminders—proof of how far we can go, and all we can accomplish together.

Greece in the spring—white buildings against bright blue skies, and the way Frank marvels at the olives like they're jewels.

"They're too bitter," I say.

"Well, I need something to counteract your sweetness," he replies, with that grin that makes my heart flip.

Ireland, where the rain comes down sideways and the hills are so green it almost hurts to look at them. We toast over pints of Guinness, and Frank slips into a questionable Irish accent for weeks after we get home, imitating the two locals—Logan and Owen—who became friends and eventually our tour guides during our stay.

Germany, where we trace the edges of old family stories and sip coffee in quiet corners, speaking softly, as if the walls remembered. We meet strangers we laugh with, and climb mountains.

Egypt, where the air smells of sand and history, and we stand in awe before the pyramids—so still, so ancient—feeling smaller than we ever have. We pull sand out of our pockets for months.

Africa, where we wake to birdsongs and watch elephants cross the road like they have somewhere important to be—followed, inevitably, by Frank's endless jokes about chickens trying to cross after them.

"Now we finally know why they're all crossing the road," he says, every time. And every time, I laugh.

We ski in Vermont, tumbling more often than not, laughing the whole way down. Frank helps me up every time, kisses my frostbitten nose, and declares us the undefeated champions of the bunny hill. I'm pretty sure I leave with bruises in places I didn't even know could bruise—but I also leave with cheeks sore from smiling.

We wander through museums and marketplaces, laugh through translation errors and lost luggage. We dance on cobblestones and kiss in train stations. We collect postcards, inside jokes, and tiny souvenirs—fragments of a world that keeps growing bigger and brighter the more of it we see together.

Each trip feels like another vow: to live, to see, to love—all while we can.

We have seven years. Seven beautiful, borrowed years.

And then comes the shift.

Time has a way of folding in on itself when you're happy. You don't realize how quickly it passes. You can blink and years are gone. It's not the same when you're in pain. Pain drags. Pain takes its time. Pain demands to be felt—it doesn't let you blink it away.

The first sign is so small I almost miss it. He gets winded on a walk we've taken dozens of times before. Brushes it off with a joke, the way he always does.

Then come the night sweats. The weight loss. The way his eyes seem a little dimmer by the end of the day. He cuts his finger when playing in the sand with the kids and doesn't take it seriously. It bleeds for too long.

We know what it could be.

We just don't want to name it.

There's a specific kind of silence that comes after a test result you didn't want to see. It presses against the walls. It fills your throat. It wraps around your chest like a weight. It takes up all the space in the room and doesn't leave any room for you to be in it. And then it creeps up your throat and spills out your eyes.

They want to keep him in the hospital.

They say his immune system can't fight this on its own. That if he stays here, they can monitor the infection more closely, respond faster if things change.

We both agree, it's for the best.

He's back in the hospital by January. Luckily, I'm still on Christmas break. When school starts up again, I call and let them know I need time. I start taking diligent notes—nurses, doctors, procedures, and their corresponding costs.

It helps me feel in control of a situation where I have none. It brings order and focus when my mind wants to spiral.

This, I can do.

He's discharged briefly. Then we're back.

There's a small black-and-white television mounted in the corner of the waiting room, the kind with thick dials and rabbit-ear antennas wrapped in tinfoil. I can't help but imagine some exhausted nurse coming back and forth to wrestle with the foil, making sure the waiting patients have something to occupy their time. The picture crackles every so often, lines flickering across the screen like static-laced snow, but it holds steady enough to make out the broadcast.

"Little luxuries," I whisper to Frank and bump his shoulder, a half-smile tugging at my lips.

He smiles, dry but amused. "Practically the Plaza," he murmurs, and gives my hand a gentle squeeze.

On the screen, Apollo 14 glides into focus, grainy footage of astronauts descending slowly onto the moon's surface. The room hums faintly with the sound of the broadcast, muffled but clear enough.

We sit quietly and watch, transfixed, the hospital spinning on around us, nurses moving in and out and stretchers squeaking in the distance.

In a strange way I feel a quiet kinship with the men on that screen—adrift, yet still tethered. Suspended between two worlds. For me, it's the fluorescent hum of the hospital, the weight of worry beside me, and the distant rhythm of a world still turning outside these walls.

For them, it's the silence of space, where they drift through the unknown, tethered to a ship, to Earth, to memory. Home is hundreds of miles away—but still, somehow, just within reach.

I can't help but chuckle quietly at how perfectly this is playing out in real time. History is unfolding in front of us as we sit here, tethered to stiff hospital chairs, waiting for Frank to be admitted. The world keeps spinning. Ours stays right here. But I suppose the world, at least to Frank and me, is in each other's hands.

We're finally called, and the same routine begins again.

Now that Frank's back in the hospital seemingly full time, the doctors mention he'll need blood transfusions. Not just one—several. Regularly.

Dr. Laszlo sits me down privately.

"Mrs. Madden, Frank's red blood cell count is dangerously low. And with the treatments he's receiving, it's only going to get harder to maintain.

"We'll need to give him transfusions—likely more than one. The problem is, we're short on compatible blood types. The supply isn't always reliable these days."

He glances at his clipboard, then back up at me.

"We're looking for donors. A positive, O positive, AB positive—any of those would help. It doesn't have to be family. Just someone willing and eligible. The sooner we find them, the better."

He softens his voice.

"I know this is a lot. But even one pint could make a real difference. If you can ask around—friends, coworkers, neighbors—it might help keep him strong enough to keep going."

I nod. My mouth is dry, my tongue feeling like sandpaper. I can't seem to find any words. But I will. I'll find the words. I'll find the people. Because if this is all I can do to help him, I will put everything I have into it.

I rally like I never have before. I call everyone I've ever met—friends, neighbors, old classmates, people I haven't spoken to in years. I'm not shy about it. I don't have time to be. I ask them to come in, to be tested, to see if they might be a match, if they might be able to donate. Mike asks around at work too, and word spreads quickly.

And then… people start showing up. People I never expected. My heart clenches at the sight of them—lining up quietly, some with coffee in hand, others holding paperwork, shifting nervously in plastic chairs. A woman from our old block. A few of Mike's coworkers. Cousins. Friends. Franks coworkers from the paper.

Our grumpy uncle Rudy even comes. I think Mom dragged him in by his ear.

Even Dad. Dad *comes*.

I didn't think he would.

I hoped in my heart he would.

Things have gotten better over the years—not perfect, but somewhere on the road to better. The air between us is still strained, like trying to see through a foggy window. The love is there, just a little clouded.

He loves Frank too. How could you not?

When he looks at me, his eyes are desperately sad. And then he hugs me the way he used to when I was little—a tight squeeze, solid and warm—and cups my cheek without saying a word.

It's not just the gesture of everyone coming—it's the time they take, the hope they carry, the way some of them pat my shoulder or squeeze my hand before walking through the double doors. For a moment, I let myself believe: maybe this is how we save him. Maybe this is the net that catches us.

Donors

1. *Me* – *AB+* —— *gave 2/11/71*

2. Mike – A+ —— gave 2/14/71

3. Rudy – O+ —— gave 2/14/71

4. Annette – O+ —— gave 2/17/71

5. Ludwig – O+ —— gave 2/19/71

6. Caroline - AB+ -gave 2/15/71

7. Patty - O+ -gave 2/10/71

8. Mom - AB+ - gave 2/15/7/71

9. Dad - B+ - can't use

Possible Donors

1. Ludwig – O+ → OK (✓)

2. Patty – O+ → No

3. Harry (sick)

4. Arlene – O+ → No (questionable, recent infection)

5. Harry ?

6. Petey ?

7. Barbara ? ?

8. Al (Mike's shop) - AB+ (✓)

9. Matthew (The Daily News) 0+ (✓)

<u>Feb. Transfusions</u>

- Feb. 12 – 1 pint (packed cells, Al)

- Feb. 14 – 1 pint (from Caroline)

- Feb. 16 – 2 pints packed cells

- Feb. 17 – due to finish

→ 1 pint Annette

→ received dose + 1 pint (Arlene? & Ludwig)

I keep track of it all as best I can. Everything. Every doctor who treats him with respect, every nurse who looks at him unkindly. We still leave notes for each other. I bring in a notepad for his room in case he's sleeping and I need to step out—or, heaven forbid, in case he can't speak.

Still, we find moments of laughter in the heaviness. He gets his first grey hair and I pluck it out with tweezers, tape it to a piece of paper, and label it: "One grey hair, found on Hubby." It earns a real laugh—breathier than I would've liked, but still a lovely sound.

"That's not grey, that's platinum. I'm just getting fancy," he says, and kisses my hand with so much love it makes my heart ache. I hold onto that moment—his laugh, the feel of his lips on my skin—longer than I probably should. Because after that everything begins to blur.

Those weeks pass in a haze of hospital shifts, beeping monitors, and bad food. I spend every hour I can at his bedside. Frank seems more tired with each passing day. He still tries to work from his bed and I laugh at him. The doctors start to talk at me, not to me—about his counts, his oxygen, how things are worsening.

Sometimes, I climb into the narrow hospital bed beside him. We laugh about one of our trips—how he made the kids laugh zig-zagging up a hill in Germany to keep them occupied. His smile always reaches his eyes, even now. We still leave notes for each other, whenever I have to leave the room so he doesn't worry or wonder.

Hubby,

I had to go bring Ma home. Be nice to the nurses or I'll switch your Jell-O to lime.
I love you,

-Trudy

When I get back to the room, there is always a note waiting for me. Sometimes he's awake, sometimes asleep, but the words are always there—scrawled in his shaky hand, waiting quietly. Even when he can't say much, he still finds way to speak to me.

T,

I'll miss you, even in my sleep. By the way, you should see your face when you're bossing doctors around. You beautiful terror.

Then, one day—a day like any other—I walk in and see one of the nurses I like is on shift as I'm going over my to-do list in my head.

1.   Report Dr. Beek to Supervisor: he saw Frank was in distress and didn't know where the resuscitator was.

2.   Find out who the night nurse tonight to stay with Frank so I can give instructions to:

-Use resuscitator

-Set suction to clear phlegm

-Where is the resuscitator? Make sure it is in clear sight for every nurse and doctor as to not repeat the incident with Dr. Beek. He was the worst. Definitely report him.

3.   Does Frank require blood today? I think the blood bank is open, but I'll need to check. Do I need to have someone come in to donate? Mike said he can come again today.

4.   Will he need blood tomorrow too? Check who's available tomorrow.

5.   Should Frank be in Intensive Care? We've had few near-misses and maybe more around the clock care is safer.

The nurse looks over and gives me a small, sad smile while I'm rattling off my internal checklist one by one. I need to write it down when I get to the room so I don't forget.

"How is he today?" I ask.

She shrugs. "Not much different."

I start to settle in—put my bag down, pull up my chair—I notice the note from when I left

Hubby,

I'm running out to grab a new notebook, this one is on its last page, and if I don't get a new one your next love letter is going to be on the back of a grocery receipt.

T-

I'll miss you like I miss good coffee, and that's saying something.

He's asleep and I'm re-reading his note, messy and barely able to fit on the last page of the notebook—when I hear it. Beeping. Louder. Faster.

Then someone yells. A code.

The room fills like floodwater. Nurses. A crash cart. Hands everywhere. People everywhere. Voices shouting numbers.

Are they hurting him? What's happening?

"Frank?" I call, but no one hears me.

"Frank?" Louder this time.

No one answers.

Someone grips my arm and pulls me back. I try to shake them off. "Let me go—he needs me! That's my husband!"

I try to get closer but they're in the way—so many bodies between us.

And then—

That sound.

The long, flat beep that makes time stand still.

His heart stopped.

And mine stops with it.

I think I'm screaming, but I can't hear it. The room tilts and I collapse to the floor, hands trembling, reaching for something—anything—that might make this not true.

I need Frank.

I need him to open his eyes.

I need him to laugh and tell me it's all some terrible joke.

"I'm sorry, Mrs. Madden. He's gone."

The words warped, muffled, like echoes from the ocean floor. A hand finds mine. A tug. Someone trying to lift me, to anchor me back into a world that suddenly makes no sense.

"Everyone get out!" I scream, voice ragged, broken. "Go away—leave us alone!"

The nurses know me by now. I'm sure there's a protocol, but I don't care.

"Please," I sob. "Please, just let me be with him."

I don't know if they leave. I can't see them anymore.

All I see is him. Still. I've always only seen him.

I climb into the bed, curl beside him, and stroke his hair— the same dark hair that made my breath catch the day he walked into my apartment, carrying a dolly and a sandwich like some kind of miracle.

"Frank, don't go. Please don't go," I whisper. "Stay here with me."

I bury my face in his neck.

"Do you remember our wedding?" I whisper. "You looked so handsome in your suit, standing there waiting for me at the end of the aisle."

My voice catches. "I would live that day over and over again."

A tear slides down my cheek and falls onto the hospital bed.

"It was the greatest night of my life."

My voice shakes now "I need you. I don't want to live this life we built without you in it. I don't know how. We were supposed to have time together. It's not supposed to go like this."

My voice cracks.

"Come back. Please… come back."

I don't know how long I lay there. Voices murmur around me, but none of them register. It's like I'm underwater, the world distorted and far away.

I feel a hand stroke my hair—gentle, like I'm a child. It's soothing. Familiar.

"*Mein liebling*," I hear someone whisper.

But I'm too tired to answer. Too lost in the strange hum that's settled over everything.

"Trudy? We have to go home."

Who said that?

I blink and see Mike. When did he get here?

It's dark outside.

"I can't leave him," I say to whoever's talking to me.

"I know," he says gently. "But it's time to go."

I lean down and brush a kiss against Frank's cheek. "I'll see you soon. I love you. I love you. *I love you.*" I will never be able to say it enough. I press my head against his forehead and whisper "Don't forget to write, my love."

I feel hands guiding me, lifting me from the bed. Then I'm in the car.

I feel the air on my face.

And then I'm home. In bed.

I turn toward the pillow beside me and breathe in deeply.

It smells like Frank. I inhale long and deep and let myself drift.

I'm untethered, without my anchor drifting into nothing. I don't know what to do with myself. I know I have to plan a funeral, that's what happens next right?

I call the funeral home and find that Frank has already taken care of everything. He planned it all. From the wake to the funeral to where he would be buried. I know he was trying to help, but now I have nothing to focus my hands on busing. All I have to do is decide the day and times but even that has limited windows. Everything is on Long Island, to be near the family he had chosen, but he will be laid to rest here, close to me. Forever. Since there's nothing I can do now, I decide to write him a letter to take with him. I'll tuck it into the pocket of his coat one last time. I know the thought would make him laugh. But it can't, because he's not here. Grief hits me like a tidal wave and suddenly I can't breathe. I'm clawing at the neckline of my shirt. It's too tight. My breath's coming too fast and my vision is spotting at the edges. My chest feels tight and hollow at the same time. I find myself on the floor, the pen trembling in my hand. "I don't know how to say goodbye. Don't make me say goodbye" I say to the room. Nothing but silence answers me.

I feel cold hands on my face and look up to see Patty's steady eyes.

"I can't do this," I manage between panting breaths.

"I know," she says gently. "But right now, I just want you to breathe."

She places an ice cube in my palm and tells me to squeeze. I do. It helps.

The world, once blurry and far away, begins to come back into focus. Her face sharpens. The noise returns. And with it, the sobs. They pour out of me—uncontrolled, unrelenting. A waterfall crashing down.

Patty strokes my hair and murmurs soothing nonsense, the kind that only someone who loves you knows how to say.

We sit like that for a long time—on the floor, in the grief, in the quiet. Eventually, I let her guide me to bed, with Smokey trailing behind us.

From there, I hear her in the kitchen, calling people, telling them about the arrangements. I let her. I have no energy left to speak.

I only know it's the day of the wake because someone comes to get me. Caroline is here now. She helps me get dressed and touches up my face.

"You'll thank me," she says. And she's right—I want to look nice for Frank. We settle on a simple black dress, cinched at the waist, falling just below the calf. I look far more composed than I feel.

I sit at the front, eyes fixed on him. It looks like Frank. But it doesn't. Still—if this is the last time I get to see his face, I will not look away. I study every line, every curve, every facet I once traced with my fingertips. I bask in the painful sweetness of these final hours together. People come. They speak. I don't reply. My eyes are on Frank. And Frank alone.

When the wake ends, they begin to close the casket.

My breath catches. A quiet, desperate panic rises in my throat. *This can't be it.*

And then they place him in the back of the hearse. I want to crawl in after him. To be near him. To stay close. To not let the car pull him away from me.

Suddenly I see her in my mind—Jackie Kennedy, walking beside that long, heavy casket down Pennsylvania Avenue.

I used to wonder how she did it. But now I understand. The need to be near him.

To stay with him until the very end.

To walk every last step beside the love of your life, even if your knees shake beneath you.

Because love doesn't stop at goodbye.

The funeral goes as funerals do. People speak, prayers are said, hymns echoed—but I barely register a word. It's held in the same church where we were married, and my mind is flooded with memories of joy: the way his hand trembled slightly when he slipped the ring on my finger, the way his eyes lit up when the doors opened and the organ swelled.

Now the same organ plays something softer, sadder. The same aisle I walked down toward forever, I now sit beside, clinging to the casket that holds what is left of it.

The priest speaks of resilience. Of carrying on. Of love that outlives the body. Of letting go after a long fight. I try to listen, I really do. But all I can do was rest my hand against the polished wood and pretend he can still feel it. I think about the letter I slipped into his jacket pocket before the casket closed. I pretend he's reading it somewhere else.

Somewhere in the distance, the organ picks up and someone begins to sing *Ave Maria*. That's when I know— it's time to leave.

I walk beside him, my hand still on the casket, and I can't stop thinking about the last time we walked this aisle. How different it was then. How full my heart was. We were hand in hand, full of hope and promise.

Now my heart feels shattered into pieces so small I don't think it can ever be reconstructed.

The place he's laid to rest is nice. Peaceful. It's in a cemetery not far from our apartment, nestled beneath a tree. He must have known I'd want to visit. That I'd need to. And he wouldn't have wanted me baking in the heat of the summer sun.

Thank you, Frank.

The thought tugs at the corner of my lips. It feels like he's left me a little love letter, tucked into the roots of this tree.

I love you, my Trudy. I don't want your beautiful skin burning in the sun. So I got you this tree, see? So you can still come talk to me if you want. You can come read your letters to me. You didn't think you could stop writing to me now, did you?

I hear his voice in my mind, soft as a caress down my spine.

And somehow, I *almost* smile.

Chapter 15

"The pain I feel now is the happiness I had before. That's the deal."
— *C.S. Lewis*

Whoever said time heals all wounds has clearly never carried one this deep.

Time hasn't softened the pain—it's only sharpened the edges, made me miss him more fiercely.

It's shown me just how lucky I was.

Time slips away; I can't tell how many days have passed. They bleed together, shapeless and endless. I write to him in journals now, as if each entry is a letter he might still somehow read. I ask him to intercede with God—to beg on my behalf—to let me come to him. My anger with God is fierce and raw. We kept the rules, did what was asked, and still He took this wonderfully good man. I can't understand it.

Line after line, I empty myself onto the page. I tell him how lonely the apartment feels without him. How quiet. How *wrong*.

March 16, 1971

Dear Hubby,

I am so lonely for you. Where are you? Can you see me? Have pity on me. I want to be with you. Tell God I want to come to you now. You can't be happy without me and I can't be happy without you. Help me. Tell Him I want to come now.

It is 12:30 now——we would be chatting over tea & cookies & hugging. You would watch T.V. in bed & I would get sleepy. I did so love our life together. You don't know the bargain I made with God——to save you, no matter what, I would care for you gladly.

You had so much to live for.

March 17

We have those flying ant bugs again——you remember them, don't you? I killed a whole nest full over by the couch.

Hubby, I can't stop thinking about you & us together. Every mannerism of yours I know so well. The blinking eyes when I caught you reading the replies, the lower lip when you were frowning. I can't stop thinking of the way you spoke with your eyes to me in the hospital and I understood. We didn't need to talk to communicate, did we Hubby?

293

We had our own language. No one knew the deepness of our world. Sure, people knew we were happy but only we knew the true extent of our happiness. It was a deep love & only death could part it.

So, God sent death to part it.

How could He take you? I don't understand.

March 18

Another day—can it be almost a month without you? Hubby, I would not have believed I could have lived this long without you. I want to be where you are. If you are dead then I want to be dead too—how do I keep living without you?

March 19

I miss you more than ever.

Death is so irreversible. I am plagued with thoughts of whether I could have done more for you.

When I read about a new drug or a new idea, I say maybe they will help Frank too, & then I remember that it is too late to help you now. Help me, Hubby...I am sure we will meet again in another world one day.

Days blur together in a haze of soup I don't finish and water I forget to drink.

My clothes hang off me now, loose and shapeless, but it doesn't matter.

I don't get dressed most days.

I call the school. I tell them I need more time.

They say maybe it's time to resign.

I say fine.

What does it matter anymore?

I only get out of bed to feed Smokey.

He lost Frank too, and he needs someone to take care of him—so I try. As much as I can. For him.

I think people are beginning to worry about me. Some offer to come stay with me, but I tell them I don't want company. At first, it's just my mother. She comes twice a week, even though I've told her not to. She puts food in the fridge and then sits on the bed beside me. I don't talk much. She doesn't seem to mind.

She hums, sometimes sings softly. Sometimes she brushes my hair or strokes it gently like she used to when I was a little girl.

Then both of my parents begin to come.

My father sits in the corner chair, quiet, worried.

My mother fills the silence for all of us—with songs, with stories, with love.

Eventually, he speaks too. I rarely respond. But still, they come.

Patty and Caroline start showing up. Sometimes separately. Sometimes together.

They make me get out of bed, guide me to the couch, tease me about brushing my teeth.

They bring me books.

They chatter about who they're dating, what's happening at work.

They laugh easily, brightly—full of life.

I resent it.

And I know that isn't fair.

After they leave, the silence closes in again.

And in those moments, I think—more often than I want to admit—that I want to join Frank.

That I want sleep to wash over me like the tide and not let me wake.

Annette comes with cakes.

Mike comes and talks about everything and nothing—filling the room with his voice like he's trying to push the sadness out with sound.

They come in rotations.

I begin to notice that.

Each time, there's food.

Each time, something to say.

And even when I can't reply, I listen.

One day Patty comes over, more nervous than usual.

She sits on the edge of the couch, twisting the strap of her purse in her fingers.

"I hope you don't get mad," she says gently. "But I asked around at work."

I glance over, wary.

She presses on, slowly. "One of the women I know—her husband died last year. She saw someone. A counselor. Not a *shrink* or anything like that—just someone to talk to. Said it helped her breathe again."

I say nothing.

Patty sets a folded scrap of paper on the nightstand, like it might bite her. "I'm not saying you have to. You don't even have to read it right now. But I thought... *maybe*."

I nod, barely. I don't pick up the paper.

She doesn't push. Just sits there a while longer, humming a little, to fill the sound. I don't know if I'll call. But I don't throw it away either.

After she leaves, I put the paper in the drawer. And go back to sleep, hoping again to see Frank.

I don't know how much time passes like this, but it feels like I've lived a hundred lifetimes in this strange stasis. Not alive, not gone—just suspended somewhere in between. Grief has bent me. I used to stand tall. Now my shoulders sag under the weight of what I've lost.

There's a knock at the door. I assume it's one of my friends or family, taking their turn on what's become an unspoken rotation. I shuffle toward the sound.

When I open it, I see a bouquet—bright, full of color, impossibly alive. A sudden burst of joy in my doorway.

The delivery man hands me a small envelope, offers a gentle smile, and walks away.

It's from Frank.

I read it like someone starved, like I've been underwater and this is air. I devour his words, my vision swimming, barely able to see through the tears.

My Trudy,

By now, things have probably taken a turn neither of us were hoping for. I know you'll want to sit in your sadness, but please, my love, don't. I remember coming home from the war in Korea and not knowing what to do with myself. I felt sadness deep into my core. The world lost its color—and you are all bright colors. Don't let this mute you. Keep living. Keep exploring. Keep laughing.

I really was hoping to stick around and annoy you into your eighties. I had big plans, Trudy—gray hair (more than just the one you plucked), matching sweaters, long arguments about crossword puzzle clues and who left the toast out. I was going to get so opinionated about the thermostat. The good news is, you get to win every argument now. The bad news is... well, you'll have to pretend I'm still chiming in from the peanut gallery. (Because I will be. Loudly. Especially when you try to put ketchup on eggs.)

But life, as you always say, has a funny way of rearranging itself. And if there's anyone who can learn to dance in a new rhythm—it's you.

Promise me you'll still eat too much strudel with your mom. That you'll keep reading those big, fat books with tiny print and arguing about them with Patty and Caroline.

That you'll keep writing those beautiful letters, even if you think no one's reading. (I'll still be reading. Ghost perk.)

Let Smokey curl up on your lap and purr while you drink hot cider. Sing in the kitchen. Put up that god-awful wall paper in the bathroom that we argued about—I won't be around to stop you.

And when you miss me—because I know you will—just look for me in the smallest things. The laugh you didn't expect. The breeze that hits just right. The way a moment feels like it's trying to tell you something. That's me, tapping your shoulder from the somewhere-after-this.

I know it hurts right now. I wish I could take that from you, tuck it in my coat pocket and carry it with me instead. But you have a heart that feels deeply because it loved deeply. And what a gift that is. What a life.

So grieve if you must, my darling. But don't let it close you up. Let it crack you open wide enough for the light to still get in. Keep traveling. Keep sending postcards. Keep writing notes and hiding them in pockets. Maybe one day you'll even fall in love again—and I hope you do. (Though, for the record, I set the bar unfairly high.)

I'll be waiting—on some distant shore, with a sketchbook and two cups of coffee. One with too much sugar. Just how you like it.

I love you, Trudy. I always have. I always will.

Yours forever and into eternity,

Frank

I read it. Then reread it. Over and over, the words Frank left for me wrap themselves around my heart like a favorite song I never want to end. I bring the letter into bed with me and hold it close, reading it until the lines blur, until I can hear his voice in every word. Until it feels like he's with me again, if only for a little while.

And then—

For the first time in a very long time—

I wake up with the sunrise.

I wrap myself in a blanket, cradle a cup of tea in my hands, and sit quietly as the colors stretch across the sky. The light breaks through the clouds slowly, stubbornly—like hope clawing its way through the darkness.

I sigh long and deep. *Okay. Three good things.*

1. I'll carry that letter with me always.
2. I have friends and family who love me.
3. … I think two is enough for today

Today I will clean my apartment. It's something small. Something manageable. I can do that, for Frank.

Chapter 16

"In the midst of winter, I found there was, within me, an invincible summer." —
Albert Camus

Every day, I've been trying to do a little—just something small to move myself forward. It still feels like trudging through mud, but Frank asked me to try, and I can't deny him. The little things add up. I notice the rotation of friends starts to dwindle, hopefully that means I'm making progress in their eyes. My parents still come though. I keep my distance from my father, but my mother continues to fill the room with love—and food.

Eventually, I start to feel like I'm coming back into my body. Not the same as before—this version is heavier, worn by grief and pain that tugs at the edges—but I'm there. The world is still muted, but every now and then, there's a color.

Every so often, I'm pulled back into the memory of the hospital. The sound of the IV fluid dripping, the beeping monitors, the quiet chatter of nurses just outside the door—it all returns with an almost unbearable clarity. Those memories are tangled in sorrow, but they're not only filled with pain. Sometimes, when I think of those days, I also remember the small mercies—the moments of grace and kindness that made the weight of it all just a little lighter.

I think moments like that—and people like that—deserve to be remembered. Too often, they go unspoken. Someone offers compassion, then carries on with their day, never knowing they made all the difference to someone else's life. We're so quick to speak when something goes wrong—but it's just as important to speak when someone does something right.

There was one doctor who offered compassion freely, unlike the others who treated it like a commodity. He saw Frank as a person, not a number or a faceless patient taking up a bed. So, with all the strength I can muster, I sit down to write him a letter.

Dear Dr. Laszlo,

I've sat down to write this letter more times than I can count, and each time the words felt too small. Grief has a way of making everything feel a little fragile—but still, I didn't want to let another day pass without saying thank you.

Frank passed away some time ago, and not a day has gone by that I haven't thought about the time we spent in that hospital, and the people who walked alongside us in those final weeks. You, especially.

You treated Frank with dignity, respect, and a gentleness that meant more than I can fully express. You spoke to him like he was still fully himself—still a whole person, not just a patient or a chart. And you treated me the same. You looked me in the eye when you explained things. You asked how I was doing, not just out of politeness, but like you actually meant it. That kind of compassion stays with a person. It stayed with both of us.

Frank trusted you. He told me once, after a particularly difficult night, that he felt safe when you were on shift—that he could rest a little easier knowing you'd be the one making decisions. I can't tell you how much comfort that brought us both.

Even in the heartbreak of it all, I carry that with me. That someone saw him. That someone cared. That someone did their job not just with skill, but with heart.

Thank you for treating him like he mattered. Thank you for treating us like we mattered.

With deepest gratitude,

Mrs. Trudy Madden

I fold the letter carefully, sealing it with shaking hands. It's the first real thing I've written since he died—something with weight, with purpose. But as I set it aside, the stillness returns, heavier than before. That's enough for today. It was something I wanted to accomplish, and I'm exhausted from it.

And that's when I realize: I can't go back to teaching—at least not children. They're too vibrant, too joyful, too alive. If writing one letter required as much energy as I just expended, how can I possibly put on my usual circus in front of a class? Besides, it's too much of a reflection of the life I had with Frank—the fun, carefree parts. The parts that now feel too far away.

I know myself well enough to understand it would only hollow me out further. After Frank died, every single one of my students sent me a card. Each one filled with love and sympathy, written in shaky handwriting with too many exclamation points and misspelled feelings—and it broke me wide open. They meant every word.

I don't think I can walk through those halls now, not with their eyes full of worry and pity. It's just too much. I can't imagine standing at the front of that classroom, pretending to be whole.

But rent doesn't wait for mourning. My savings are thinning, and I need to figure something out—*soon*. Because as much as I want to hide under the covers and wait for the ache to pass, life keeps knocking. And it doesn't knock gently.

Teaching still feels right, in some form. Just… maybe not the same way.

I call Patty and Caroline. My voice shakes a little when I ask if they can come over. They don't hesitate—not even for a second.

"We'll be there tonight," Patty says, as if she's been waiting for the signal.

"I'll bring ice cream," Caroline adds. "And wine. And five thousand ideas."

They show up like a burst of light, just like they always do. Caroline kicks off her shoes the minute she walks in. Patty hands me a bouquet of daisies from the corner stand and kisses the top of my head.

Caroline does bring ice cream—three flavors, because she can never decide—and a container of tiramisu, which we used to order whenever we went out together. It's Frank's favorite, not mine. Always was. I used to tease him about his "sophisticated sweet tooth," and he'd grin like it was a compliment. I feel my throat tighten as I lift the lid. The cocoa dusting, the soft layers—it's like a postcard from him. A quiet reminder. I swallow hard. It's not just dessert. It's memory. It's love.

Maybe this is his way of saying, *Good job, Trudy. Now have a treat. You're on the right path.*

And somehow, that thought loosens the tightness in my chest. I smile. It's small, but real.

"I'm just glad to see you upright," Caroline says, gently.

We sit in a circle on my worn living room rug, papers spread out, wine glasses full, and heads bent together like schoolgirls making a plan.

They toss out ideas between sips and laughter—some serious, some ridiculous.

"You could tutor," Patty suggests. "Private clients. One-on-one. Less noise, more control."

"Or a dance instructor!" Caroline exclaims, eyes suddenly wide with mock inspiration. "That's still teaching, right? Let's get your body moving again!"

Before I can object, she's already on her feet, grabbing my hips with both hands and swaying us around the room like we're on stage at Radio City.

She's laughing—head thrown back, wild and unapologetic—and despite myself, I start laughing too.

"Okay, okay, Martha Graham," I say, breathless between giggles. "Let's not get crazy. This rug is vintage."

She twirls me once more for good measure, dramatic and ridiculous, before plopping back down on the floor, satisfied.

"Just saying," she grins, reaching for her wine. "Busy body, less busy mind."

Patty raises an eyebrow. "Is that a real saying, or did you just make that up?"

Caroline shrugs dramatically. "Does it matter? It should be."

I smile, the warmth of it surprising me. The ache is still there—it always is—but it's softened by their company, by this moment. The frenzy of friendship, playfulness, and hope baked together into a quiet light I can carry with me, even after they leave.

"Or adult education classes!" Patty chimes in, trying to keep us on track. "Community centers always need instructors. You wouldn't have to pretend to like dodgeball *ever again*."

I laugh—*actually laugh*—and it feels foreign in my chest, like something I haven't worn in a long time but still fits, somehow.

There's something appealing about teaching adults. It feels like I'm closer to Frank somehow. We always did what we could to help those who needed it. That feels like a good starting point.

I interview at community centers and women's prisons. Eventually, I hear back from a women's correctional facility—they're offering me a position teaching literature. It feels right. It also feels wrong not to be able to tell Frank about this new shift in my life, this big change I'm making. I wonder what joke he would've made, if he'd be proud, what books he'd recommend we study. I smile at the thought.

The job isn't something I love—it doesn't give me the same purpose teaching children did—but it passes the time and pays the rent. It keeps me moving forward, even if the steps feel small.

Through it all, the calendar flips onward, indifferent to how tightly I cling to the moments behind me. I don't like having new memories without him, but somehow, this feels like the beginning of making them.

There's a shift that happens then. I start to move a little more. The ache is still there—of course it is. I carry it with me everywhere I go. But I'm trying. I'm leaving the house more. Living more. And yet, every now and again I get reminders of the time before. Today it was a letter I stumbled across back from when Frank was still alive, tucked inside the pages of a book. I look at the date and try to blink myself back into that time, from when we were still married, back before my world broke apart. I wrote to Robert Kennedy, another quiet moment of trying to change the world.

ROBERT F. KENNEDY

NEW YORK

United States Senate

WASHINGTON, D.C. 20510

February 20, 1968

Mrs. T. Madden

50-10 65th Street

Woodside, New York

Dear Mrs. Madden:

Some time ago, you were kind enough to write to me about the violence and disturbances in our cities, and give me your views on the need for more law and order in our urban areas. I appreciated hearing from you and regret that I was not able to acknowledge your letter when it arrived.

No one condones the violence which erupted in our cities last summer. A violent few cannot be allowed to threaten the lives of the majority. Those who riot, and those who incite to riot, must feel the full force of the law. In my judgment, however, strengthening of law enforcement procedures, while valuable, should be only a portion of our response to this situation. I think we must also take action now to alleviate the causes of hopelessness and frustration which prompt ghetto residents to riot. I am deeply convinced that we are not doing enough to break the vicious cycle of poverty in which many of our citizens are trapped. All of us — business, government, concerned citizens throughout the land — must make a greater commitment to helping the poor to reverse these distressing trends, by making available better jobs and improved education and housing for our fellow Americans. Indeed, because I believe that government programs alone are not adequate to meet the problems of our cities, I have introduced legislation to promote private enterprise participation in the tasks of rebuilding our nation's cities — in providing both housing and jobs for ghetto residents. I hope that I shall have your support for their enactment.

Again, my thanks for your views on this important matter.

Sincerely,

Robert F. Kennedy

Robert F. Kennedy

I feel like it's another nudge from Frank, *remember who you used to be, my love. Don't let her go.*

I'll try to find her again, Frank, or this new version of her at least. I promise.

I can't help but let the memories take over—visceral and real. What life was like back then, and the way I felt compelled to write to the senator. Frank had made writing letters feel so easy, so natural, it became second nature. I saw what was happening in the world and I wanted my voice to be heard, to matter in whatever way it could.

I couldn't look out my window and ignore the unrest. I couldn't see what happened in Detroit—that eruption of despair and rage, one of the deadliest riots in our country's history—and do nothing. I couldn't watch the police brutality in Newark create divides people couldn't unsee.

The Long Hot Summer of 1967 sat heavy in me, as it did with so many others. And I couldn't sit idly by. All of this—layered with the protests against the Vietnam War—was a powder keg. Everyone could feel it.

I remember sitting down to write to Senator Robert Kennedy, my hand trembling with the weight of all that needed to change and had yet to be done.

September 20, 1967

Dear Senator Kennedy,

I don't know if this letter will ever reach you—or if you'll have the time to read it—but I hope it does, and I hope you will.

I'm a schoolteacher from Queens. I live in a neighborhood filled with families from all over—Polish, Puerto Rican, Irish, Black, Italian. Every morning I greet children whose parents work long hours and come home tired, just trying to keep the lights on. I see how hard they try. I see what they carry. And lately, I see how scared they are.

The violence this past summer was horrifying. But what frightens me more is how easily people are blaming it on the poor, the young, and the voiceless. My students aren't criminals. They're hungry. They're tired. They're trying to make sense of a world that often tells them they don't belong in it.

We need peace, yes—but we also need understanding. We need housing that doesn't fall apart around them. We need teachers who don't give up. We need jobs with dignity. We need hope. We need compassionate policing. Police officers that see the public as people and will treat them humanely and with dignity and respect.

You've spoken about these things, and it gives me courage. I wanted to write and tell you that there are people out here—ordinary

314

people——who believe in the work you're doing. We're tired, but we're still here. And we're listening.

Thank you for fighting for those who are too often forgotten.

Sincerely,

Mrs. Trudy Madden

Just a few months later, he was gone. Shot, like his brother before him.

I remember how the apartment went quiet when I heard the news. I turned off the radio. Then turned it back on. I couldn't stop shaking.

It felt like losing something personal—someone who had seen the same cracks in the world and dared to speak them aloud.

I made a point to keep that letter. Tucked it between the pages of a book I'd forgotten about until today.

Sometimes I wonder what would've happened if he'd lived. What kind of world he might've helped build.

But mostly I remember that moment—when I was a young wife in Queens, writing by lamplight, tired and scared and trying to make sense of everything. And how, for just a moment, my voice had reached someone. I remember showing Frank. I was so proud that he'd answered, that my

315

voice mattered. "Of course it does," he'd answered, as if it was the most obvious thing he'd ever heard. As if I was the most important person in the world.

I can't help but get lost in a whirlwind of those memories—of our marriage, our life, and its eventual end. I'm brought back to that moment in the doctor's office, when we found out about his diagnosis together. Clinging to each other like we could somehow hold the pieces in place, keep everything from falling apart with just the strength of our grip.

Then the rage hits. Hard and hot, rising up my chest like a fire I can't put out.

That doctor.

That inconsiderate, cold doctor who told me to leave Frank—so I could have babies. As if that was the only value my life could hold. As if love wasn't enough.

The anger finds its way into every corner of me. I feel it humming under my skin, settling into my bones, taking up residence in every cell of my body. And I don't know what to do with it.

My eyes land on the letter I received from Robert Kennedy all those years ago, still sitting on the kitchen table. Without thinking, I sit down, pick up a pen, and begin to write again.

But this one's not for a senator.

This one's for *him*.

Dear Dr. Johnson,

I've thought about you often these past few months——far more than I ever wanted to.

I should have said something to you that day. When you looked me in the eye and suggested I leave the man I loved because he was sick. When you handed me a cold diagnosis and followed it with colder advice. As if his illness somehow made him less worthy of love. As if I were foolish, naïve, or selfish for staying.

But I was in shock. I couldn't speak. I just sat there, clutching the arm of that hideous chair like it could anchor me, trying not to fall apart while the world was breaking open around me.

So now I'm saying what I should've said then.

How dare you?

How dare you suggest that I should have walked away. That I should have abandoned a man who, despite everything, loved me more fully, more honestly, and more joyfully than anyone ever has. That I should have chosen a life of comfort and safety over five minutes——five seconds——of what I had with Frank.

You saw his chart. I saw his _heart_.

You looked at numbers. I looked at the man who made me laugh on the darkest days, who held my hand through every storm, who painted snowflakes for my niece's birthday like they were masterpieces. ~~He was joy~~. He was ~~light~~. He was mine.

And you told me to leave him.

Maybe you think the only meaningful contribution a woman can make in life is her ability to bear children—but Frank saw more in me than that. He saw my mind, my spirit, my stubbornness, my drive. He never once made me feel like I had less to offer just because our path might look different. He made me feel whole.

Perhaps you felt your advice was practical. That it was meant to protect me. But it wasn't. It was dismissive. It was cruel. And worst of all, it was <u>small</u>.

Because love—real love—is anything but small.

He's gone now. And my grief is bottomless. But I do not regret one single second. Not the pain. Not the fear. Not the end. I'd do it all over again ~~without hesitation~~.

So next time—if there's a next time—think twice before you tell a woman to walk away from love just because it might hurt. Love always hurts eventually. But if it's good, if it's real, it's worth it.

Frank was worth it.

And I will not let anyone——least of all you——diminish that.

Sincerely,

Mrs. Trudy Madden

I stare at the letter.

For a half a moment, I consider not sending it. Just writing it felt cathartic—like I'd finally exhaled something that had been lodged in my chest for a long time.

But then I think: if this gives him even a moment's pause before saying something like that to another woman—or man, for that matter—then it's worth it.

And besides, it felt damn good to write. It was a gentle release of the grief I'd clutched so tightly for so long—like finally loosening my grip and letting a little of it drift out into the world.

Grief, I've learned, is like the ocean. Some days, the water is calm, and I can stand there, looking out at the depth of it all. Other days, the waves are so violent I can barely keep my head above water. And then there are days when I think I'm fine—until a tidal wave crashes down without warning.

I hold on to the days I feel fine—well, as fine as I can. Because I know what's creeping behind corners are the days I can't breathe, where I'm drowning in the grief that keeps trying to pull me under. I remember one summer day at the beach—Mike, Annette, the kids, and me. It was a day I thought I was doing okay. I sat in a lawn chair, letting the sun warm my skin, toes buried in the sand, the sky soft and blue above me. The waves rolled in and out like a metronome. For a while, everything felt steady. The waters of my grief seemed calm.

Denise wandered over, quiet and thoughtful, her hair damp and her eyes focused. She held out a small shell, turning it in her fingers. "Uncle Frank would've liked this, wouldn't he?" she asked.

And just like that, the tidal wave hit.

I couldn't breathe. Karen, always watching with those steady brown eyes, came over and gently wrapped an arm around Denise.

"Come on," she said sadly. "Let's go build a sandcastle, like when you were little."

I didn't wait to see if they walked away.

I ran into the house and collapsed onto the bedroom floor. My breathing was ragged, my vision blurred at the edges. But the difference now? It ebbed away faster than it used to. I suppose I could call that progress.

The next day, I made a point to rise with the sun.

I needed to see the hope in the clouds.

I needed to exhale my grief into the morning air and breathe in something new—something that felt like a beginning.

I wrapped my hands around a warm cup of tea, watching the steam spiral upward. It felt like my grief was rising with it—real, thick, and warm—intertwining with the sky above.

I thought of Frank. Of what he wanted for me. I thought about our love. Our love was like fireworks at the top of a Ferris wheel. Bright. Colorful. Lighting up the night sky— and then gone in an instant. But the colors stayed, stained behind your eyelids, and the memory—on your heart forever.

He wanted me to keep seeing color. To keep finding beauty. To keep living.

And I'm trying.

"It's just so hard sometimes," I whispered into the wind.

A breeze stirs the air, soft but certain. As if Frank is answering me. *I know, my love. But you have to try.*

So I do.

For him.

For me.

For us.

Epilogue

From that point on, my life was spoken of in three seasons: before Frank, during Frank, and after Frank. The hardest truth is that most of my years unfolded after him.

But life moved on, as it so often did.

I never stopped looking for Frank though.

I searched for him across every inch of the Earth, sometimes alone or sometimes with friends. He and I truly felt like we tucked our love into the world, embedded it in places that needed to be found, so I kept looking. I looked as if I might catch a glimpse of him in the curve of a distant hill or hear his laugh echoing between cathedral walls. I walked the Great Wall of China with the wind in my hair and imagined him beside me, hand shielding his eyes, marveling at the scale of human persistence. I ran with polar bears in the wilds of northern Canada—while thinking how Frank would have made some ridiculous joke about the bears offering hugs.

In Antarctica, I danced with penguins in a clumsy shuffle on the ice, making me laugh loud and free—the cold pinching at my cheeks like he might if he were teasing me. I rafted down the whitewater of the Teton Mountains, clutching the sides with one hand and his memory with the other. In the Galápagos, I watched sea lions laze in the sun and thought of the afternoons we used to do the same, quiet and content with nothing more than each other's company.

I read novels on park benches in London, pigeons fluttering at my feet, and imagined him stealing bites of my scone. I stayed in an ice hotel in Norway and thought how we would have laughed as we shivered, and how the tip of his nose would have turned pink in the cold.

I wept when the northern lights appeared in Iceland—so bright, so strange, so achingly beautiful beneath the Icelandic sky. "He would've loved this," I whispered to the sky. The feeling reminds me of my sunrises.

I wandered Berlin before the Wall came down, feeling the tension in the air, a city divided yet pulsing with hope. Frank would've had thoughts on that—political ones, of course—but also something soft and human to say about people on opposite sides trying to love each other anyway. In Ukraine, I traced a path through villages I'd only heard of in family stories, lighting a candle in a quiet chapel and saying his name aloud in the silence.

I didn't find him, not exactly.

But in every place, I found a version of us—what we might have said, how we might have kissed beneath foreign skies, what he might have ordered at a small café. I collected those moments like postcards from the universe. Frank wasn't in one place. He was in all of them, folded into every step I took forward, every sight I saw through tear-brimmed eyes.

And somehow, that made it easier to keep moving.

I went back to school—because learning had always been a way forward for me. I needed something to tether myself to, something that challenged me, that reminded me I was still capable of growing.

I earned my second master's degree, and over coffee one day, I told Patty I was thinking about medicine. She blinked, then smiled that wide, knowing smile of hers. We talked through what it would take—how long, how hard, how many doors I'd have to knock on just to be taken seriously in a field still so heavily dominated by men. But I knew, deep down, this was the path I needed to follow. It took a long time, but it felt so good to work towards something and to achieve it. So I went back to school: four years of medical training, a year of interning, then three more in a grueling anesthesiology residency. It was exhausting, both physically and mentally, but it gave me purpose. And through it all, I saw Frank in every patient. In every chart I read, in every quiet breath before surgery. It was as if caring for them was a way of still caring for him. I gravitated toward anesthesiology—something about it felt right. Quiet, precise, and deeply human. The kind of work no one saw but everyone depended on. Like Frank.

Eventually, I found my way to the VA hospital. Surrounded by veterans, I felt closer to him than I had in years. Their stories echoed his, their strength and weariness so familiar. It was like coming home in a strange and steady way.

I worked harder than I ever had. And over time—through years of sweat, study, and proving myself again and again—I became head of the department.

It didn't bring him back. But it brought me purpose.

A few years after he died, I read a piece in *The New York Times* about something called CHOP—a new chemotherapy regimen showing real success. *Real cures.* I clipped the article, then couldn't bring myself to read it again. It felt like looking through a window into a life we might have had—if the timing had been just a little different. If we'd had just a little more time. It reopened a wound that I'd been healing. I spent a few days in bed after that, recalling those days in the hospital.

I kept up with Dr. Lazlo over the years. He wrote back after I sent that thank-you letter—it touched him that I'd taken the time, and we ended up corresponding quite often after that. It turns out he'd caught the metaphorical travel bug too. We sent postcards back and forth, swapping stories of our adventures like old friends trading secrets.

I met Jackie Kennedy once. Not in any grand or showy way—just quietly, in the corner of a party in Manhattan. The coming together of two widows who understood something wordless. We didn't take a photo. We didn't need to. We simply talked. It was lovely—soft and sad and somehow comforting. A brief, gentle moment of being seen by someone who knew the weight of carrying on.

And yes—I loved again. Or something close to it. I dated a few men over the years, but Frank, as always, was right. He'd set the bar very, *very* high.

I spent nearly a decade with one man. Eight full years. But things never settled quite right. We didn't fit the way love is supposed to fit—not like I'd known it could. It was warm, but not lasting. Familiar, but not home. Eventually, we parted quietly, and I went on alone again. Not lonely. Just… aware of what real love had been. I spent four years with a different man, but we weren't right either. But they were good at helping pass the time. He was much more wrong; I affectionately referred to him as regrettable but not disastrous.

I continued my quiet activism. Not with marches or headlines, but in letters and donations, in votes and conversations that mattered. I wrote to congressmen. I sent money when I could—to shelters, to causes Frank and I both believed in. I kept a stack of magazines by the door—*Ms., The Nation, Catholic Worker*—and left them behind in waiting rooms or passed them to friends. Small things, maybe. But consistent. Quiet didn't mean passive. I even made a point to include donations in my will—gifts to the causes that meant the most to me. A final act of love. Of conviction.

I adopted more cats over the years. Always strays, always needy. Smokey lived a long, spoiled life, curled up beside me through seasons of sorrow and healing. I used to joke that Frank was sending them to me, one by one, to keep me company. It's the kind of thing he'd do.

I stayed close with Patty and Caroline, and we kept up our book gatherings which we eventually called book club—meeting every month without fail, or at least every other if life got in the way. We read everything from *Jane Eyre* to racy romance paperbacks we'd pretend to be embarrassed about, but always had plenty to say. Our discussions usually started out civilized and literary but almost always spiraled into heated debates, laughter, and a second round of cocktails. We didn't just talk about books—we talked about the world, the latest causes we wanted to support, the news, the men who drove us crazy, and the lives we were still figuring out. The books gave us an excuse to gather, but it was the friendship and the shared sense of purpose that kept us coming back.

Caroline found a man who matched her zany, chaotic energy—someone who could keep up with her wild ideas and laugh until their sides hurt. Patty fell for a doctor who was calm and steady, the kind of man who listened more than he spoke and made her feel safe just by being near.

They both married in beautiful ceremonies—Caroline's bursting with music and color, Patty's quiet and elegant, full of gentle smiles and soft light. I was there for both, proud and full of love—and aching, deeply. Not with envy, but with the weight of remembering. Of knowing what it felt like to love that fully. To have had it once, and to miss it every day since.

Mike and Annette stayed by each other's side for sixty-four years. Their love was quiet and steady, teasing and loud and the kind that hums in the background of a life rather than shouting from the rooftops. Together, they raised a family, hosted holidays, and showed me what enduring partnership looked like. Annette eventually found her natural mother. The search took years, but in the end, they found each other. As it turned out, Edith had been searching for Annette too. They didn't have forever, but they made the most of the time they were given—grateful, at last, to no longer be strangers. When they met, it was as if they'd never been apart, even though sixty years had passed. From the moment she arrived, Edith was part of the family—and she remained so until the day she passed. I think it healed something in both of them—like two parts of a heart finally becoming whole.

Michael Jr. met a kind woman. Together, they carved out a path rooted in service and compassion. He used his brilliant mind to help others, and they traveled the world side by side, doing missionary work and giving their lives to something greater.

Karen—sweet Karen—loved deeper than anyone I've ever known. She found love young, in a boy she hadn't been looking for. A boy who carried too much on his shoulders, mischief in his eyes, and a heart that gave without ever asking for anything in return. I saw it before she did, I think. He made her laugh until she cried, and held her when the tears came from somewhere else. Their love was a beautiful thing to watch unfold, it started with the embers of friendship that turned into a blaze of a love true and deep.

Theresa was still wild and free, always chasing the wind. She loved in bursts—intensely, bravely, and sometimes heartbreakingly. She lost and loved again, a heart that refused to settle for anything less than everything.

And Denise—clever Denise—was always sharper than people gave her credit for. She, like me, craved adventure and to see the world. She loved someone who was wrong, and then, in time, someone who was beautifully, undeniably right.

The girls all had children of their own, bringing joy and noise and new life into our lives again. It felt like the world expanded, in laughter and little footsteps. And Mike—true to his word—finally started that book club, but for them. He'd talk about stories and characters with the kids and toss a wink in my direction like we were in on a secret.

There were Christmases and Easters. And ordinary days, too. The quiet ones in between that made up the real substance of a life.

I stayed close with Mom. We lost her in July of 1979. The world dimmed without her humming in the kitchen, without her steady warmth filling a room. Dad followed in 1989—on Easter, of all days. It felt strange for it to be Easter. Poetic, in a way. Like it closed the door on that long-ago argument we never quite came back from.

We never fully mended things. Our relationship was always a little fragile, a little strained. But in his final moments, he asked for me. He wanted to know if I was there.

I was.

Not in the room, but close. And maybe that's the best way to describe us—not fully near, not fully far. Just... somewhere in between.

Eventually, I started to feel weaker. The doctors told me it was Parkinson's. Slowly, my hands began to tremble, and the small things—the buttons, the teacups, the pen start to slip from my grasp—but not love, never love. That, I held onto with everything I had.

Whenever it is my time—when my feet finally stop their shuffling, when the sun rises without me—I hope it finds Frank and I together again. Somewhere warm. Somewhere with cats and coffee and a view of the ocean.

Until then, I'll keep watching the sky.

I'll keep writing.

I'll keep loving.

Always and eternally,

Trudy

P.S.

Trudy passed on Father's Day, at 82 years old.
There was something poetic about that—like the quiet closing of a chapter left open far too long. In her final days, she spoke of seeing Frank in her apartment, and of Mike, who had passed six months before, ever protective, watching to be sure her journey was safe. Always connected in life, their bond endured even in death. Her parents, too, appeared close in her thoughts, speaking to her, as though all of them were calling her home—or perhaps to that beach, the one with the coffee and the sunrise.

Her funeral was held in the same place where she once said goodbye to Frank. The same place she married him. All she ever asked was to be with him again. And so, she was laid to rest beneath that old tree—their tree—right beside him.

Finally, together again.

She had so desperately wanted to be reunited with her love, but she lived a full life while she waited.

She mourned him, yes. But more importantly—she *lived* for him.

Dear Aunt Trudy,

I knew you, of course—but I never knew you in that time before.

People always talked about what you were like then. Big. Bright. Bold. You had to have been, to have done all of the things you had done and accomplished. You broke down barriers and smashed glass ceilings. You made a difference, in your own way. You didn't need to stomp your feet and scream and shout.

Through your letters, your journals, and this story, *while still fiction*, I feel like I've caught a glimpse of the woman everyone spoke about. And in the small moments you shared with me—your clever jokes, your faraway stories— I saw flashes of her too. Though imagined, I hope these pages carry a truth of spirit, even if it's not in fact.

When I knew you, you still lived life out loud... just a bit more quietly.

So, thank you. For letting me know that version of you— it's been a gift.

For helping me understand the love you felt.

For making sure we could all feel it—that love, brief and bright like fireworks across a night sky.

And now, I think you've been given the gift you wished for most:

For Frank to live eternally with you, here on the page.

I hope that brings you peace.

Love you,

Laura

P.S. Maybe you and Grandpa can add this one to your book club. xoxo

About the Author

Laura DiTieri writes character-driven fiction rooted in hope, family, and resilience. Inspired by her great-aunt's letters and family history, her debut novel, *Don't Forget to Write*, is a heartfelt exploration of love and loss, infused with humor and heart. Laura is passionate about bringing stories to readers everywhere; as a lifelong reader who overcame early struggles with dyslexia, she went on to earn a double major in Early Childhood and Childhood Education with a minor in English, and later a master's degree in Special Education. Her years of teaching deepened her belief in the power of words to connect people across generations. When she isn't writing or wrangling kids, she can usually be found with a book and a cup of tea—dreaming of the day she'll finish it before it gets cold. She is currently at work on her next novel, where magic and romance collide in unexpected ways.

www.ingramcontent.com/pod-product-compliance
Lightning Source LLC
Chambersburg PA
CBHW021957130726
47903CB00014B/1620